THE HUNTER AND
THE HUNTED

Spur refined his sight, tracked his target past a patch of brush, then squeezed the trigger.

On the lead horse, Matthew Rorick seemed to sense the shot. He looked straight ahead at the split tree, started to raise one hand, then the heavy, .52 caliber round smashed into his chest, tore through his heart, and exploded out his back, splattering Jamison with blood.

Rorick slammed off his horse and onto the ground. His arms flew wide, and he tumbled over onto his back, his eyes staring straight upward.

Now the hunter became the hunted again.

Also in the *Spur* Series:

SPUR #16

RAWHIDER'S WOMAN

DIRK FLETCHER

LEISURE BOOKS NEW YORK CITY

A LEISURE BOOK®

September 2004

Published by

Dorchester Publishing Co., Inc.
200 Madison Avenue
New York, NY 10016

ISBN 0-8439-2365-2

Visit us on the web at www.dorchesterpub.com.

SPUR #16

RAWHIDER'S WOMAN

ONE

In the year 1875 a good man could work ten hours a day for twenty dollars and "found" on a cattle ranch or as a hired hand on a farm. A clerk in a store might draw down twenty-five or even thirty dollars a month. That's a yearly income of $240 to $360. President U.S. Grant was in his second term in the White House, and the first nine inning no-hit baseball game was played in Philadelphia, Pa.

The twenty-cent piece was authorized this year as a silver coin, and the first typewritten book manuscript was completed by a relative unknown, Samuel L. Clemens. He called it, "Adventures of Tom Sawyer." The transcontinental railroad had been completed for six years and Isaac Charles Parker took over the position of judge of the Federal Court of Western Arkansas. Judge Parker at Fort Smith became known as the "hanging judge."

Will Jamison hitched up his pants, settled the .44 New Model Remington army revolver on his hip and glanced at his two sons beside him. Will was a tall man, six-one, lean and stringy with a brown drooping moustache and now a four day's growth of beard he hadn't taken the time to shave off. His clear green eyes checked the street again, then he nodded and stepped into the Willow Creek Fiduciary Bank.

The boys, Dale and Phil, were slightly smaller versions of their father. Behind them Matthew Rorick pulled up a red and white bandana from around his throat and covered his face right up to his eyes. The three ahead had done the same thing.

Will charged up to the waist high metal cage, pushed aside a woman customer and waved his pistol at the surprised male teller.

"This is a stickup!" Will bellowed. "Everybody raise your hands and shut up!"

Dale and Phil leaped across the barrier and ran to the two teller cages. Quickly they took out all of the paper bills there, then grabbed the man sitting behind the president's desk.

"Open the safe!" Dale bellowed in much the same angry tone of voice that his father had used. Dale was softer, twenty-eight, smaller and lighter. He also had a sandy drooping moustache. He jabbed his six-gun in the man's face.

"Move! Get the vault open or you're dead right now!"

The bank president, Aloysius Nestor, groaned as he rose from the chair. Dale slammed the heavy revolver across his forehead and jerked him forward with his left hand.

"The vault, dead man, now!"

Nestor cringed, then walked stolidly forward to the vault. He stepped inside first, grabbed a loaded pistol from the rack near the door and turned trying to aim it at the vicious gunman in back of him. It was too far to turn. Nestor was too slow and clumsy. He tried to pull the trigger.

Dale shot him through the throat. Nestor went

down with a gurgling scream. The shot in the small vault echoed as the sound slammed around and around, deafening Dale. He ignored the drumming in his ears. It had happened several times before. He watched Nestor drop his weapon and crash to the floor. A growing pool of blood puddled the vault. Then Nestor whispered something and died.

The blood pool stopped growing. Blood never flows from a body after the heart stops pumping it.

Dale Jamison stepped over Nestor and began pulling out drawers in the vault. The third one was stacked with paper money. He fished out stacks of banded bills and pushed them into a brown cloth sack he carried. He rushed as he cleaned out the first drawer, found three more that contained paper money. He emptied those also, passed over stacks and sacks of gold coins.

Early on the Jamison gang had learned that gold was valuable but ten pounds of it was worth only $3,300. Ten pounds of twenty-dollar bills could be worth three times that much. They never took gold unless there was no paper currency.

"Hurry it up in there!" Will Jamison barked from outside the vault. He held two pistols now, staring down a dozen workers and customers. "Everybody sit down!" he barked again, this time at the customers and clerks. "Down on the floor! Do it right now!"

The customers sat slowly. Rorick pushed down two older men who were having trouble getting on the floor.

Phil Jamison walked around making sure everyone was sitting down. He had his weapon out, an old Colt. He was good with it, but his dad said he always wanted to shoot too much. Privately Will called Phil a bloodthirsty sonofabitch, but he never told him that to his face.

Phil snarled something at a pretty girl. She

blushed and turned away. He reached down and cupped one of her breasts where it bulged against her dress. She edged away. Phil laughed.

Roger White had sat down with the others. Now he was sweating. In his pocket he carried a Derringer, a two-shot loaded with .45 rounds.

What was happening here was wrong. He knew that. He should be doing something about it. Damnit! He had to do something! He eased one hand around and pulled the weapon out when the robbers looked away. Now he held the small weapon between his legs where he had crossed them. The younger robber looked at him, scowled and then looked away. He carried only one gun. But the older robber was closer.

White had sworn to Mr. Nestor that he would help protect the people's money. If the robbers got away with this, half the people in town would be broke, bankrupt!

Roger watched the younger robber touching Lucy. He had been sweet on her for a year now. They kind of had an understanding that when she was a year older they would be married. He hated it when the kid touched her breasts. He had never even touched them! It drove him wild.

He had to do something! There was no one else. That's why Mr. Nestor had bought the Derringer for him. He had to use it now!

Phil caught the girl's face in his hand. "You be good to me, big tits, and I'll be nice to you." He reached down and squeezed one of her breasts.

Roger felt a cold sweat break out on his forehead.

"Nooooooo!" he screamed, lifted the Derringer and fired at the molester who touched Lucy.

His shot missed from eight feet away and smashed into the wall.

Will spun, the big six-guns both coming up. He fired one round from each weapon. The first caught

Roger in the chest, punctured one lung and slammed out his back. The second round hit almost at the same time as the first and drove through Roger White's black suit coat, through his shirt and shattered a rib before it cut a deadly path through his heart and lodged against his rear ribcage.

Two women screamed.

Roger jolted backward by the impact of the two .44 rounds. His head hit the floor with a crack, but he was already dead. His eyes blinked open and stared unseeing at the ceiling.

"Don't nobody trying nothing else foolish!" Will bellowed. "That fool died for trying it. Anybody else does the same thing gets lead poisoning. You understand?"

Heads nodded in shock and grief. Unbelieving eyes looked at the dead body of what only a minute ago had been the most popular teller in town and the best church soloist the little Baptist congregation had ever had.

Dale came out of the vault. He had two brown sacks crammed with banknotes.

"Done!" he said.

The four robbers backed toward the front door. Phil was out first. He turned casually as he had done so many times and slid his weapon against his thigh as he watched the street. Nobody had noticed the robbery. Good. He nodded to Gabe Hinckley who had been on guard outside. Gabe's rifle stood innocently beside his leg where he leaned easily against the brickwork of the best bank in town.

Inside, a six-gun roared again and a man passing the bank looked up, then began to run. Gabe Hinckley grabbed the rifle, a Henry repeater, and swung it by the barrel. The heavy stock hit the running man in the right shin, breaking the bone in two places and dumping him on the boardwalk. He screamed. Gabe kicked him in the head, saw that the others were out of the bank and ran for his horse.

Across the street the hardware store owner Fred Jones heard the scream and saw his friend hit with the rifle. He grabbed his Winchester 1866 model from behind the counter, ran to the door and slammed a round through the open door at the man with the rifle by the bank who kicked his friend on the sidewalk.

Jones took more time with his second round and sailed it through the tough's right leg, trying to bring him down, not kill him.

Gabe went down with a scream of pain. He had no idea where the round came from. Before he could move, another round from up the street dug into his chest and he fell flat on his back.

To Gabe it seemed everything had slowed down. He saw the other four members of the robbery gang leave the bank, leap on their horses and ride toward him on their planned route out of town.

"Will!" Gabe screamed. "Will, help me!"

Will and the other three had started firing behind them, driving two gunmen back inside storefronts. Will rode toward Gabe, saw his bloody chest and shook his head.

"Got no time to nurse you, Gabe," Will said. His .44 came down and he blasted a round through Gabe's right eye, then spurred his horse as he fired three more times behind him and the four horsemen pounded down the street, turned up an alley and were soon out of sight.

Behind them, the dazed little town came back to life. People looked cautiously from doors and windows. Then a few men came out. Sheriff Victor Adams used up ten precious minutes gathering a posse. He used three of his deputies and four volunteers. Finally they were riding, each man with rifle and pistol.

But it had taken ten minutes to get moving. The

robbers were two miles down the trail by the time the posse kicked up dust out of town.

Back in the bank two women had fainted. Three bodies lay on the floor. The woman who had pulled away from Phil Jamison's touch was the third victim.

"She pulled away from that filthy man and shouted at him," one of the men customers in the bank said. "Then the bastard ripped open her blouse and laughed as he shot her twice in the chest." The man looked at her body and tears crept into his eyes. He never noticed that he had blood splatters on his new blue suit.

In the vault, Aloysuis Nestor lay on his back, his blood soaking his jacket and a packet of one dollar bills. Dale Jamison had dropped them, evidently deciding they were not important enough to pick up.

The cashier of the bank, the number two man under Mr. Nestor, shook his head at the tragedy. Tears stained his cheeks and he wiped his eyes and blew his nose. His voice was barely a whisper.

"They won't catch them, not unless Will Jamison wants them to. That had to be the Jamison gang. I've been reading about them in the St. Louis newspapers. They had it all planned out. They must have had one man outside." He shook his head.

"Sheriff Adams certainly will not catch the Jamisons, that's a fact." He stared at the bodies a moment, then wiped his eyes again. "Will somebody go fetch Harley the undertaker? We're going to have four funerals tomorrow."

The trail that stretched south of Willow Creek was not as defined as some others. This track led to the Indian Territories, a huge area north of Texas and west of Arkansas where the Federal Government had brought in six or eight Indian tribes from the east and southeast and dumped them. The land was supposed to be theirs.

Will Jamison always scoffed at that idea.

"Damn Indians don't deserve nothing!" he roared. "Push all the fucking heathens into Mexico. Hell, I kill every one I see!"

Now he turned and checked his riders. His two sons were jolting along just behind him, Rorick was close. Not bad for a haul, he decided. He had lost only one man, and he wasn't family so it didn't matter so much. Gabe should have been more careful.

From what Dale said there must be thirty thousand at least in his brown bags. One of them rode tied to Will's saddle horn.

Christ he was glad they didn't try to carry that much gold away! They would be burned down by the posse by now.

Rorick had hung back and spotted the posse coming. He left the last little rise behind them and gave Will the word.

"Looks like six or seven of them. Riding hard, Will. But they got to be a mile behind us."

"Far enough," Will said grinning. "About time we taught these shitcake posses a lesson!" Will roared. "Teach them a damn good lesson."

He rode on scanning the trail, and came to what he wanted a mile down the path. It was a rocky ledge where a small stream cut through. The ledge lifted twenty feet on each side of the creek. The trail elbowed through the cut next to the creek. Any buggy or wagon going through would have one set of wheels in the water.

Will put Dale and Phil on one side and he and Rorick went on the other side of the cut. They hid their horses and then slithered up so they could peer over the top of the grassy, rocky ridge.

It made Will remember the war. Christ but that

had been exciting! He'd never lived so high or had so much fun in his life. Too quick the fighting was over. The killing was over. Will shook his head in wonder. He never would understand it, but in the heat of battle he went wild. He counted more Bluebellies dead than anyone in his unit. Every time.

His bayonet was always bloody at the end of a battle. He loved it! War was the greatest game man had ever invented. The only trouble was that a man had trouble finding others to play. Now he had a pale substitute.

The look of stark terror in the banker's eyes! The way the customers jumped to obey his commands! It was power, raw, life and death power and he reveled in it.

He saw a puff of dust on the downtrail. Will squinted his eyes and watched closer. They were coming. A good mile and a half away, and trotting, he figured. They would be making six, maybe seven miles an hour. Fifteen minutes they would be at the cut. Fifteen minutes and half that posse would be dead.

The idea of it surged through him and he checked his rifle. He lay on his stomach and as he watched the riders come, he fondled his Henry repeater, aware of his growing hardon. Christ, he was at it again! Yeah, this would be a good one, they always where when he got his cock up. He licked his lips and sighted in on the moving figures.

The gun motion gave him a surge of sexual feeling and he knew the jism was rising, getting ready to surge forward.

"Won't be long now," he told Rorick. "Remember, you have the second man into the cut."

Rorick nodded and laughed softly. "Gonna get me a lawman today!" he said and laughed again.

The boys on the other side of the cut knew their targets. This way they would not all shoot at the same man.

Dale rose up on the far ledge about fifty feet away and waved. He saw them coming too.

The posse stopped a hundred yards out from the cut, all grouped around and talked excitedly. Then one man yelled at them and rode hard for the gap in the ridge and they all followed. They were spread out by the time the first man hit the cut. Will waited until he was almost through to put the others in range. Nobody would fire until he did. He had taught his unit that much.

Will sighted in, led the lead rider two clicks and fired. The Henry spoke loudly and the lead man pitched forward as the round took him in the side and drove him off the thundering sorrel.

Will worked the lever and cranked a new .44 caliber slug into the chamber.

He heard rifles crack from both sides of the cut. The first four men through the gap were hit, two of them on the ground, a third one fighting to stay in the saddle, and a fourth slumped over and gunning out the other side.

The rifles spoke again and again. Three of the posse turned and fled back the way they had come, sending ineffective pistol rounds toward the concealed men on the little cliff.

The "battle" was over in twenty seconds. Will sent one more round thundering after the retreating riders, missed and moaned in delight as his hips slammed four times against the hard ground where he lay. He panted for a minute as the climax powered through him quickly and he turned to Rorick.

"Good day's work. Get your horse and run down that last sonofabitch who got through. Give him another dose of lead poisoning!"

Rorick yelped with pleasure and raced down the slope for his mount. Will and his sons checked the carnage below. Dale raced ahead, picked up a Spencer repeating rifle and two six-guns. Phil found two good rifles, a Winchester and a Lee, and they checked the men. All three were dead and their horses had run off. They would go back to town.

"Hell, don't worry about the horses. We got better mounts than they ever thought of getting. Check them for cash and watches, then let's move out. No rush now. No damn posse gonna come near us before we hit the Territories."

Dale scowled and looked at each dead man again.

"None of them has a badge on," Dale shouted. "I thought we was gonna get us a lawman today!"

"Hell, Dale, they all lawmen," Phil said. "They got to be deputized 'fore they can ride on a posse. Them guys is all deputy sheriffs of whatever damn county we're in."

Dale snorted. "Hell, I wanted me a badge. None of these fuckers got a badge!"

Will cut it off with a round from his Henry into the air.

"Enough of this caterwauling! We done it good. Now let's get the hell out of here and into the Territories before somebody else comes along."

Rorick rode back a few minutes later, met them at the horses and held in his hand a shiny silver star.

"I got myself a fornicating sheriff today!" he yelled.

"Lucky bastard!" Dale screeched.

Will stared them both down, turned his horse down the trail. It was no more than half a day into the Territories. He grinned.

Once they crossed into the Indian Territories there was no sheriff or town marshal who had jurisdiction. It was a beautiful haven for all sorts of hard-assed characters. But no lawmen. Once in a while a U.S. Marshal came around, or one from Judge Parker. But more of them were buried in the Territories than Parker would ever know about.

Will kicked his mount and moved out faster. He was anxious now to get to their hideout and see if anybody had found it and was trying to claim it.

He fingered the Henry, half hoping some claim jumper had tried to stake out his concealed cabin.

TWO

Spur McCoy rode into Willow Creek, Mo. about noon the day after the bank had been robbed.

He had guessed right. For two weeks Spur had been following the track of the Jamisons. His assignment had caught up with him at a small railroad line in Missouri where they had a telegraph office.

General Wilton D. Halleck, his boss at the Secret Service in Washington, D.C., was a man of little humor. When the secretary of the treasury upbraided him about the rash of Western bank robberies, the retired army man fired off orders to every agent he had East and West.

Spur still had his telegram in his pocket. It read:

SPUR McCOY ROCKFORD MO

DROP ALL PRESENT ASSIGNMENT STOP CONCENTRATE ON WILL JAMISON AND HIS GANG OF BANK ROBBERS STOP LAST KNOWN TO BE IN EASTERN MISSOURI STOP IF CONTACT MADE WIRE AT ONCE

19

THIS OFFICE SO MORE MEN MAY
BE SENT STOP THIS IS YOUR PROB-
LEM, McCOY SO SOLVE IT STOP

Spur threw his reins around the hitching rack in
front of a hotel and pulled his saddle bags, blanket
roll and small carpet bag off the saddle and carried
them into the hotel.

At least he figured it had to be a hotel. It was the
only one in town, two stories, unpainted, but with a
sign out front that said: *"Rooms 25 cents a night.
Bath extra."*

There was no one behind the small desk in the
lobby that was less than ten feet wide and half that
deep. He rang the bell but no one came. Spur found
the register, signed his name and left a one dollar
greenback beside his name. He wrote the room
number 16 on the edge of the bill, took key 16 from
the rack behind the desk and went down the hallway
to his room.

It was grim, but better than sleeping on lumpy,
hard ground as he had for the past three nights.

There was a bed with blankets and sheets that
would remain on the bed for the length of his stay, a
small wash stand with the usual porcelain bowl and
big rose-decorated porcelain pitcher filled with tepid
water. There was no dresser or chiffonier. The walls
were covered with the worst looking wallpaper he
had ever seen.

He dumped his gear on the floor, pushed it under
the bed but let the Spencer seven-shot repeating
rifle lie on the hand made comforter.

The Spencer was his favorite all around rifle. It
weighed ten pounds and was forty-seven inches
long, but it was hard to beat in a close in, wide-open
firefight. It had saved his skin more than once. It
held seven rounds in tubular magazines, and one

more round could be kept chambered for a total of eight.

That was eight shots compared to the Henry's thirteen rounds. But over thirteen rounds it was no contest. Spur would have two or three of the long thin tubes loaded with rounds ready to slip into the Spencer that would keep firing. The Henry had to be loaded one round at a time by hand.

He stretched, took off his dusty brown shirt and tossed it on the bed, then scrubbed his face, arms and torso with the tepid water and dried himself on a big soft towel. Spur put on his "dress up" shirt from his carpetbag but didn't bother changing his pants.

He had a midday dinner in the hotel dining room, then talked to the undertaker. The man had put four bodies in the ground that morning and was exhausted, but richer. He had four more funerals slated for the next day.

The coroner, Harley, told Spur what happened, and that the services for the sheriff and the three members of the posse would be tomorrow.

Spur did not reveal his official status, nor did he bother checking in with the acting sheriff, the lone deputy who had not ridden with the posse.

Spur next talked to an officer in charge at the bank. He explained that the bank had been declared insolvent. He said that all available monies would be paid out to depositors on a percentage of the dollars owed, as soon as the total assets were gathered.

His name was Norton Dunlap and he was the only living officer of the bank. He sat at his desk, one down from the larger one the president had used. The front door was closed and bolted. Spur had come in the back door after persistent knocking.

"You said it was the Jamison gang," Spur questioned. "How are you sure?"

"The bunch was moving across the state. I read about it in the St. Louis papers. We should have been warned. Why weren't we warned?"

"Your town has no telegraph, Mr. Dunlap. There was no way to warn you, or to know which way the gang might turn. I rode in here by chance today hoping to get a reading on their next move."

"Now you know, and now the residents of Willow Creek are the losers of forty-three thousand, two hundred and twenty-eight dollars. That's more money than this whole town is worth. I work for thirty-five dollars a month, do you realize that, Mr. McCoy?"

"You said they took no gold?"

"That's right. There were drawers in the vault opened that contained over ten thousand dollars in gold coin. None of it was gone. They wanted only paper money, it's light, easy to transport, especially when a posse is chasing you. When are we going to get some protection from gangs like this?

"The Jamison gang has robbed twenty-six banks as of two weeks ago. The St. Louis paper said they had killed over thirty people in those robberies. Now you can add three more bodies to their bloody record."

"One of the gang was killed during the robbery, is that right?" Spur asked.

"True. Our sheriff wounded him, and then Will Jamison himself shot his own gang member because he didn't want to nurse him on the trail. Also I figure he didn't want to leave any witnesses who might talk."

"Mr. Dunlap, I would like to guarantee you that yours will be the last bank the gang will rob, but I can't do that. I am on their trail, and it's my job to capture, or kill them, but I can't say just when that will be."

"Good, I hope you kill them all," Dunlap said. He

lifted his brow and wiped moisture from his forehead. "Yes, I know, that kind of talk is not very charitable, not Christian at all. But I don't feel charitable after seeing Roger White and Lucy shot down in cold blood. It was the most brutal, terrible thing I've ever had to watch."

Spur turned his hat around in his hands. "Mr. Dunlap, I can only say I'm sorry. I'll do what I can. Thanks for your help." Spur went to the back door where the banker let him out quickly.

Spur McCoy walked down the alley to the street. He was a big man for the day at two inches over six feet and weighing two hundred pounds. The weight was toned, supple muscles that let him walk with the lithe prowling quality of a big cougar. He was in superb physical condition and used to the hard life of the saddle and camping out.

Reddish brown hair showed under his low crowned gray Stetson, and full sideburns grew well below his ears. Green eyes peered curiously at the Wild West where he had sworn to protect and uphold all laws, federal, state, and territorial.

His hands were hard, but did not show the rope burns, callouses and scars they would have if he was a working cowhand. But he was good on a horse, with a rope, and had spent time rounding up and driving cattle.

Right now he was on the trail of some ammunition. He turned in at the general store and went to the back where he saw a gun rack. On the shelves lay boxes of cartridges. He picked out two containers of .45 rounds and two boxes of the longer .52 caliber loads for his Spencer rifle.

When he looked around for a clerk, he saw only a woman behind the counter. She was tall, probably five feet eight. Her long black hair fell over her shoulders and down her back.

"Finding what you need?" she asked, a smile

coming naturally, unaffected.

"Yes. Have it right here. Do you work in the store?"

She laughed and he liked the way her eyes twinkled and the way she appraised him.

"You could say that. I also own the mercantile." She checked the ammunition boxes, added up his bill and he paid it. She put the shells in a small paper sack and handed it to him.

"You're new in town, talking to people about the bank robbery. Which makes you either another bank robber learning his trade, or a federal lawman. I'd guess the latter."

Spur pushed his hat back on his head and looked at her. She had an attractive face with a slightly sharp nose, penetrating brown eyes and a rounded, full figure.

"Do I pass inspection? Or do I have a hook and eye unfastened somewhere?" She was laughing at him with her eyes.

"No, nothing unhooked and everything is in place. You are an attractive woman. In fact you're the prettiest lady store owner I've ever seen."

"Because I'm the first. I know that old story. How would you like to have a nice home cooked meal for a change instead of that old hotel food?"

"Are you suggesting that I go to a boarding house?"

"Not really. It's closing time, and I live in back. If you'll snap the night lock on the front door I'll close up and see what we can find for supper."

"Isn't that taking quite a chance?"

She frowned for a moment, put her hand to her chin, then in a darting move drew a Derringer from the top of her dress and aimed it at him.

"I don't believe in taking chances." She smiled and lowered the small, deadly .45 two-barreled weapon. "Besides, I'm a good judge of men. I hardly ever make a mistake that way." She watched him and smiled. "Hungry?"

"I'm getting hungrier by the second." Spur turned, went to the front door and engaged the lock, then came back to the counter. She had lit one lamp which she carried as she waved for him to follow her.

The rear door of the storeroom for the mercantile opened into an attached five room house that fronted on the alley. It was comfortable, clean, well furnished and pleasant. It definitely had a woman's touch.

"This is home," she said. Then she held out her hand. "I'm Ester Cooper. My husband ran the store here for ten years, then caught the shakes one day and died two days later. Our doctor had no idea what was his trouble. I've been running the store myself for the past three years. If you're counting, I'm thirty-one years old and not ashamed of it. No children."

Spur took her hand and was surprised by her firm grip.

"My name is Spur McCoy. I am a federal lawman but I would appreciate your not telling anyone. I am delighted that you offered me a home cooked meal. I'll even help do the dishes."

She smiled and went to the kitchen. "I think I'm going to like you, Spur McCoy. Ever peeled potatoes?"

Two hours later the meal was over, the dishes done and everything put away. Spur held a drink of whiskey and branch water and watched the pretty woman who sat on the couch beside him.

"I'd weigh three hundred pounds in a month if I ate all my meals here," Spur said.

Ester smiled. "Thank you. I think a man should eat. I love to cook and like even more seeing someone enjoying the food." She looked away, then stared at him. "I'd guess you're not going to be in town long."

"Have to leave at sunup. I'm after the Jamison gang."

"Oh damn!"

He looked at her quickly. He was not used to hearing women swear. She grinned and lifted her brows.

"I know, nice ladies are not supposed to use bad words, but sometimes I do. Our relationship had been moving along so well. I do like you . . . now you're leaving before we even get to know each other."

She looked away, then back at Spur. "I'm not the kind of person to sit around and wait for things to happen. And I am not bashful about going after something I want."

She slid closer to him, leaned in and kissed him on the cheek. "If you'll turn around I'll show you exactly what I mean."

Spur turned and she put her arms around his neck and drew his face toward hers, then kissed him hard on the mouth. She broke it off, leaned back and looked at him, then kissed him again, this time with her mouth open, her tongue washing his lips. They came apart moments later.

"Mr. McCoy, we don't have much time. I would be ever so thankful if you would make love to me, right now."

She caught his hand and pressed it against her breasts. She watched him, then kissed his lips again and this time his mouth was open as well and she moaned softly, pushing closer toward him, trapping his hand between them.

Spur could feel the heat of her body through her clothes. Her tongue battled with his for a moment, then withdrew and let him penetrate her mouth.

She leaned away from him, pulling him with her as she lay to the side on the narrow couch. He was half on top of her, the kiss continuing.

His hand moved on her soft flesh and she moaned again, then one of her hands unsnapped the top of her dress and she pushed his hand down inside.

Her mouth left his and she whispered to him, her voice heavy with wanting him.

"Spur, you don't know how long it's been! I always have liked making love but now it's been almost three years! I knew when I first saw you that you were the one. I'm so much in need that I can hardly sit still. You do understand, don't you? I wouldn't do this for just anyone. You are something special, and big, and wonderful!"

Spur let his hand wander through the fabric until his fingers found her warm flesh. Her breast was more than warm and when his hand closed around it she kissed him quickly.

"Yes, wonderful Spur! Yes! That feels so wonderful. Oh, yes! I love that. It feels like it did the first time a boy ever touched my breasts. At first I was shocked and upset and then on top of that came the most wonderful, warm, marvelous feeling, and I didn't ever want him to stop touching my titties. Then my father came out on the porch and the boy pulled away and a minute later he left and I had to go inside."

She pushed him away gently.

"Let's go into the bedroom," Ester said.

The bedroom was small, decorated in soft pink with a four poster bed and pink canopy, pink bedspread and three pink satin pillows on top.

She sat on the bed unfastening the buttons on the top of her dress. She paused.

"Spur, how much do you know about women?"

He sat beside her, kissed her gently on the mouth, then shook his head.

"Woman is the most complicated animal God ever invented. I'm usually at a dead loss."

"As you seduce them, you're wondering how and why. Not too likely." She kissed him back, shrugged the dress off her shoulders leaving her chemise in place.

"Most women like to be loved, but they want the cuddling, the petting, the soft, lying words, the hugging and all the tenderness they can coax out of a man. A woman exchanges sex for love. Did you ever think about that? A woman gives in to sex after she has been cuddled and petted and told how wonderful she is.

"Men put up with a little petting and loving and holding in order to get to the sex. True. So this is going to be a long, slow process." She tenderly patted the bulge behind his fly. "Big man, you just take it easy down there, and wait your turn."

She shifted her skirt and pulled the dress off over her head, then lay on the bed in her chemise and long, silk, loose drawers that came to her knees. She patted the place beside her.

"Come and lay beside me and hold me and pet me and tell me how wonderful I really am." She grinned. "Of course you're going to have to lie a lot, but I bet when your thing down there is hard and ready and a girl is half undressed, you're one of the best liars around."

Spur lay beside her, kissed her eyes, then her mouth and bored his tongue deep inside her. Then he put his arm around her and drew her to him.

"Frankly, Ester, you are a marvel. You are tall and sexy and have big breasts and you're honest about sex. That's rare in a woman these days." His hand covered her breast through the chemise, then crept under it and found her bare flesh warm and inviting. When he touched her nipple it was already stiff and pulsating with hot blood.

"Oh, yes!" Spur said. "This is going to be a wonderful night. I have right here in hand a generous, sexy woman who has a great body and fine, full breasts."

She scowled, reached up and kissed him.

"Darling Spur, talk dirty to me, use all the bad words ladies aren't supposed to hear, like cock and cunt and fuck. I like that!"

Spur did. For fifteen minutes he teased her and coaxed her and petted her breasts and got her chemise off and talked her into sitting up. Her full, heavily nippled breasts thrust out beautifully. He kissed them and chewed on them until she could stand it no longer.

"Get your clothes off, Spur McCoy! I want it right now! Push your big cock into me as hard as you can!"

She undressed him, tearing at buttons and pulling off his boots, then his pants and underwear until he was naked. She had kicked out of the long legged silk panties and lay beside him, eyes half closed, her hands fondling his genitals. She wailed and pulled him on top of her.

Slowly she spread her legs, and lifted her knees offering herself to him. Her vagina lips were pink and swollen, the wetness showing that she was more than just ready.

Spur went between her legs and eased forward, penetrating her and driving in deeply. She gasped and then smiled and lifted her legs around his neck. A soft purring sound came from her as she thrust her hips upward as far as they would go, crunching their pelvic bones together.

"Oh, God yes!" she said. "Now that is good fucking!"

Spur thrust three times and she climaxed. Her whole body vibrated and series after series of spasms pounded through her big frame. She tensed and rattled and her voice raised in a soaring wail with each new series of shakes.

Spur waited for her for a moment, then the pressure caught up with him and he slammed hard into her, driving her hips deep into the feather bed on the springs until at last he could hold it no longer and he erupted in a jolting series of thrusts that spewed his seed deep inside her.

On the last few thrusts she lifted to meet him and they both grunted in surprise at the force of the meeting. After the last mighty thrust he dropped half on top of her, half on the bed and panted to feed his oxygen starved system.

"Glory, glory, glory!" she said softly. "It has never been that good before!"

"Three years," Spur said.

"Well, not exactly three since I've had a lover. Still it has never been so dramatic, so beautiful. Never with anyone else, not even the first time."

They rested for a few minutes then sat up.

"You're staying the rest of the night," she said. It was not a question, not an order, just a fact.

"Yes," he said and kissed her.

They lay back down and he put his arm around her shoulders and she cuddled against his warm body. They talked, as strangers often do when getting acquainted. She told him where she was born and raised, and how she had come from Ohio in a covered wagon with her family, out on the frontier! He had settled for southwestern Missouri. It was already a state, and there was land to be homesteaded.

The day Ester was sixteen she got married to John Cooper who had just opened a new mercantile in the small town of Willow Creek, ten miles from her father's farm.

"I was young, and inexperienced. John taught me everything, first about sex and making love and how to be a good wife. I wanted to learn, but I was disappointed in sex the first year or so. John had no idea that a woman was supposed to climax too. He thought only of himself."

Spur told her about his early life growing up in New York City where his father was a prosperous merchant and importer. He told her wild stories about his days at Harvard University in Boston and his graduation. Then about his working in his father's firms for two years and going into the Civil War as a second lieutenant in the infantry.

"Before the war was over, I was a captain, and my friend, U.S. Senator Arthur B. Walton of New York, asked me to come to Washington, D.C. to be his military aide. The Army said of course.

"Then in 1865 the U.S. Secret Service law was passed and I applied to be one of the first agents. With the senator's help I was accepted, and here I am."

They got up and had a snack, but before the food was gone they were touching and holding each other. They never got out of the kitchen that time, making wild, shouting love on the rough boards of the kitchen floor.

Twice more that night they became one, and before dawn they lay holding each other.

"I'll never let you go," Ester said. "I may just get my Derringer and shoot us both so we can be together forever in heaven."

"But what if there is no heaven, only a long sleep without dreams?" Spur asked.

"Then I won't shoot us, and I'll hope you'll stay another day or come back and see me every week or so."

"Whenever I can." He kissed her and reached for his clothes.

"At least I can seduce you with breakfast. Hate to see a grown man go to work without a hearty breakfast."

It was hearty. Flapjacks with fried eggs on top, biscuits and gravy, hash brown potatoes, coffee, jam and toast and a firm hug and squeeze before he headed for the hotel and his gear.

At the door she put his hand down the front of her robe so he could touch her breasts.

"Spur McCoy. You promise me on your Secret Service badge that you will come back."

"I promise," Spur said. He squeezed her breast and kissed her deeply, then he walked out the door. It was time he got on the trail of the robbers. They would not be expecting anyone to be trailing them two days after the robbery and massacre. That would be his advantage.

THREE

Spur rode due west on the track that led toward the Indian Territories. Scarcely two miles out of town he came on the site of the ambush. A dead horse lay to one side of the small creek where a million flies buzzed around it. Hawks and crows had been at it, opening huge bloody landing zones for the insects. Everyone fed on the surprise meal.

There were cartridge cases in the roadway where the ambushed posse had been attacked. He found dark pools which had once been blood that soaked into the dirt. Farther along the trail he found another shootout and more of the dark red-black stains on the ground.

It was a military operation. Will Jamison must have been in the big war. He was putting his training on how to kill to a practical if highly illegal use.

Spur watched the tracks, and soon saw all of them fade except four that moved straight ahead toward the west. These would be the four Jamison gang members. They were making no effort to hide or conceal their direction or route.

33

They knew no other posse would come after them. They would soon be across the line . . . into the Territories. No Missouri lawman could touch them in the Territories.

But Spur McCoy could, and he would. It also was prime killing ground for the bounty hunters, those strange individuals who enjoyed tracking down and capturing a wanted man like some game animal. Most of the posters on wanted men read "Dead or Alive," and every one was a sure death warrant for the fugitive, whether he was guilty of not. A body slung over a pack mule or a horse was much easier to handle than a live prisoner.

Spur pushed all thoughts out of his mind and moved forward. He had supplied himself from Ester's store and now had a sack of provisions and minimum cookware tied over the carpetbag in back of his saddle. He had no idea how long he might be in the wilderness that was Indian Territories.

He had been in it once or twice before. It was off limits to settlers, but some white men had set up houses, scratch farms, and a few cattle here and there. All such uses of Indian lands were illegal, but usually little was done about violators. The place was a new refuge for all kinds of outlaws, since state officials and lawmen could not chase them inside the Territories.

There would be no hotels, no friendly farmers, no support if he ran into trouble.

Spur kicked his horse into a faster walk and stared ahead. He could see little difference in the lands: broad central plains, with a few gentle hills and rolling lands. There would be no marked change when he went across the state line from Missouri into the Territories.

He had never agreed with what the federal government had done with the Indians, especially those on the east coast that were marched out of their homelands and walked hundreds of miles and tossed into the Territories with little support, supervision or help. Congress called it "removal."

The removal of the Indians dated back to 1838 when the first of more than 60,000 Indians began the trek to the Indian Territories. The Cherokee, Chickasaw, Choctaw, Creek and Seminoles were all rounded up at gunpoint and marched across the plains from their wooded homelands to the mostly treeless prairie beyond Arkansas and above Texas.

Spur had heard stories that one of every four Indians who began the long march died on route from dysentery, measles, whooping cough or some other "white man" minor ailment.

Spur watched the rolling land and knew that sooner or later the emigrants would want to take even this away from the first Americans and use it for farms and ranches.

It was not his fight, not at the moment anyway. He saw a crude sign ahead and rode up to it. It had been hand lettered with a paint brush on a long board a foot wide and nailed to a sturdy cedar fence post. It said:

"Howdy! Your arse is safe here, this is Indian Territories! No lawmen allowed. Bounty on U.S. Marshals . . . $50. On Judge Parker deputies . . . $100. Welcome!"

Spur checked the tracks, leaning out of the saddle, looking over the now faint imprints on the ground. The same four horses he had been following went through the border into the Territories. The gang was safe, now the men would relax and move to their hideout, or set up a new one.

The tracks continued west along a little used trail for a mile, then turned sharply south, cutting across a broad rolling plain that extended as far as Spur could see. It was grasslands, with a few small rises, and a brush bordered creek snaking here and there in every direction as the water sought a route down the slight tilt of the land.

Near one small stream he saw a dozen Indian tipis. He circled around them, cut the trail again and saw that it bore almost due south. They were heading for a given point, and all the time they were coming closer to Fort Smith, Arkansas. That was Judge Parker's jurisdiction. He was the new Federal judge who had as his special responsibility crimes committed in the Indian Territories. Quickly he had become known as the hanging judge.

Spur rode all morning, paused in a small copse of trees for a quick drink from a stream and ate the sandwiches Ester had made for him. She was a delightfully interesting person. He just wished he had more time to get to know her better.

Spur had one more drink from the pure little stream, then leaned back just as a rifle bullet slammed through the space where he had been and splashed into the water. He dove to the side and rolled toward a fallen tree. Three more shots came in rapid succession all from the left where a small rise gave the gunners the advantage.

His rifle was still in the boot on his saddle where the horse stood a dozen paces away. Two more rifle slugs slammed over him, pinning him behind the log. All they had to do was run around to his flanks and nail his carcass to the log. He fired twice over the log, but the gunners were out of range of his Colt .45 pistol.

He knew he had to move, and made a desperate dash for his mount, but six rifle slugs drove him back to the log.

For a moment there was silence, then a different sounding weapon boomed from fifty yards above the first ones, on up the small rise.

Spur could not see any of the shooters. The newer weapon that sounded like a Sharps barked four more times, and there were only two return shots from the lighter sounding rifles below. None of the rounds were aimed at Spur.

A man surged around a rock and raced down hill twenty yards, then slid behind a scraggly tree and waited. One shot came at him, and he put three more slugs into the area where the ambushers had been. He stood and fired once more, then watched for a moment.

Spur could hear the sound of horses as someone moved away at a gallop.

The man on the slope above tried one more shot, then cradled his weapon across his chest and led his horse down the hill toward where Spur still lay behind the log.

When Spur looked over the log again, the man had stopped thirty yards up the hill.

"Hello down there. Don't shoot. I'm one of the good guys. I'm coming into your camp." He slung the rifle over his shoulder with the barrel pointing down and walked the animal down the hill.

Spur checked him out as he moved. He was tall and thin, wore clothes that had been on the trail for at least two weeks. Black hat, a Sharps rifle, and a six-gun on his hip. His boots had spurs that jangled as the horse moved.

When the rider got close enough, Spur saw that he was just a kid, no more than seventeen, maybe eighteen. Blond hair fell down the back of his neck. He wore thin leather gloves and pulled his bay up ten yards from Spur.

"Friend," he said lifting both hands when Spur rolled over and came up with his Colt .45 pointing at him.

"Is it all right if I get down?"

"Whenever a man saves my life, I let him alight and introduce himself," Spur said, standing. "My name is Spur McCoy."

37

The kid slid off the horse and held out his hand.

"They call me Longjohn Ferrier. I know about you. You're hunting down the Jamison Gang. I figure you could use some help, since your odds are four to one. With me on your side it would be two to one, much better odds."

"True." Spur shook the hand and tried to evaluate the young man. "Thanks for getting me out of a jam. They had me pretty well in a hole there."

"Yeah, they did. But old Matilda and me knew what to do." He patted his Sharps-Borchardt rifle. "This old girl scared off two of them and wounded the other one. Bunch of rawhiders from the look of them. You got to be more careful traveling alone in this country."

Spur nodded. He had heard about the new Sharps-Borchardt, a single shot rifle that fired a .45 center fire round. But the thing was a half inch longer than four feet and weighed nine pounds.

"I've been here before," Spur said. "The fact is I work alone, not looking for a partner."

Longjohn grinned. "You lawmen never are. How did I know you was packing a badge? The way you look, the way you ride. You're too damn clean to be living out here. There's still even a woman's perfume smell on you. I wasn't trying to be your partner, teacher would be more like it."

Spur scowled and started to reply.

"Let me have my say. Out here you look like a lawman, every killer and petty thief in the Territories is gonna be gunning for you. Nothing personal, nobody out here likes the law, and especially federal lawmen. Get dirty or get dead."

Spur nodded, realizing the young man had a good point. "You got any other free advice?"

"Lots of it. First off, don't ever stop or camp in an open place like this, makes you a sitting duck. A man out here will kill you for your horse, saddle and your guns. He don't need no other reason. You gonna be here a while, suggest you toughen up a little."

"Thanks, that *is* good advice."

"Also, watch your backtrail better."

"What?"

"I saw you in Willow Creek, been following you ever since. Good thing I was friendly."

"And you're interested in the Jamisons?"

"A mite bit, yes. Four of them got wanted posters out. There's two thousand dollars a head on them four."

"Dead or alive?"

"That's the ticket! Neater, cleaner, that way," Longjohn said.

"And you aim to collect?"

"Hell, a lawman like you can't collect no reward. Might as well be me as anybody."

Spur nodded. "Might as well, but don't look for any help from me."

"Real neighborly. After I saved your ass just now."

"I didn't need all that much help."

"You took it."

"Not much I could do about that. How old are you?"

"Old enough. I've collected three bounties already, five hundred each. All alive when I turned them in, in case you're wondering."

Spur put his gear together and mounted up.

"Free country, Ferrier. Man can ride any trail he wants to around here. I can't stop you."

Longjohn pushed his light brown hat back on his forehead and rubbed his chin with his hand covered with the skin-thin leather glove.

"You shore don't sound none too friendly. Maybe you just don't like bounty hunters."

Spur nodded. "You could be right."

"We serve a purpose. No way enough lawmen to bring in all the riff-raff that is running around, especially here in the Territories. I've heard some bounty men hunt guys down like animals, kill them on sight. I never had to do that."

"How old are you, Ferrier?"

"Old enough. Eighteen."

Spur laughed. "More like sixteen."

"Yeah, well I'm over seventeen by two months. If a man is big enough, he's old enough. I can pull a trigger and shoot straight. That makes me just as big and as old as the next guy."

Spur turned his mount and rode south. He cut across the trail again after a ten minute search.

Longjohn Ferrier rode behind him.

"You ain't much on friendly," the young man said.

"I am with friends," Spur said.

A mile on south Longjohn was still there.

"You know anything about the Jamisons?" Spur asked him.

"Bank robbers, killers. Robbed over thirty banks by now and probably killed more than thirty people. Usually they kill one or two at each bank. Favorite targets are lawmen."

"You been shot at before?"

"Lots of times, like today."

"Which way did those guys you rousted head out?"

"North," Longjohn said.

"Good, I don't need no extra trouble. I didn't come down here to fight every outlaw in the Territories."

"With two we could stand guard at night," Longjohn said.

Spur lifted his brows, threw up one hand in defeat.

"You know how to fast track?"

"Of course," Longjohn said.

They galloped their horses down the long, shallow valley for half a mile, then each made a hundred hard arc round the center of the valley, trying to find the tracks of the four horses.

Longjohn found it first and whooped. Spur rode up, checked the tracks. They were at the far side of the valley, and soon they angled up and over the low rolling ridge. They followed slowly, but when the tracks headed down the next valley south, Spur and Longjohn nudged their mounts into a gallop again for a quarter of a mile, then they checked the ground the same way.

An hour before sunset they had moved what Spur guessed was fifteen miles. The trail led over another small rise and to the left they could see a fair-sized Indian village.

"Everything peaceful with the injuns," Longjohn said. He lowered a pair of old army binoculars. "Seems strange. Most guys would have raided the place for a young girl if nothing else. These guys all hate the Indians."

"Which means they were in a hurry, and maybe they were close to their hideout."

Before they could move from the cover of the trees, gunshots echoed up the valley. They saw two white men on horses charging the Indian settlement. To their surprise, the small Indian village went to ground, the women and children vanished into tipis or into brush, and six braves dropped behind log barricades and began shooting at the charging raiders.

One of the attackers took a round in the chest and slammed off his horse, hit the dirt and rolled half a dozen times before he stopped. His horse veered off from the shooting and soon vanished down the valley. The second white turned back toward his partner, stared at him on the ground for a minute, then seemed to shrug, dropped down and took the pistol from his holster. He mounted and rode off into the brush at the end of the short valley.

"Maybe that was why the Jamisons didn't hit the village," Spur said. "Some of these red men are learning how to protect themselves from raiders."

They rode on. Spur not pleased that the bounty hunter was with him, but for the moment he could not think of a good reason to send him packing. He had a point, two men were three times as effective in this lawless land than one man alone. It might work out. He would try it for a day or two and see. Spur McCoy had no thoughts of helping Longjohn to get any reward. He didn't even want to think about it. If it happened, it happened.

By dusk they turned into a thicket, found a small clearing and built a fire. Longjohn had a full sack of supplies. They ate canned beans, had a mess of potatoes, and bacon along with their boiling hot coffee.

When the food was gone and gear cleaned, Spur left the fire going, built it up a little and then took his horse and his rig a hundred yards into the thicket.

Longjohn began to follow him. Spur stopped and looked at him.

"I thought you were an experienced man out here in danger territory," Spur said.

"I been here before."

"Good. Then you know not to sleep near your campfire. That smoke is a beacon for five miles for anybody smelling it. You go on the opposite side of the fire. If anyone comes, one of us should hear them."

"Yeah, yeah. I was just about to ask you if I should do that." Longjohn scowled as he turned, walked his mount past the fire to the brush on the far side and kept going.

Spur could have ridden away from him right

there, but he decided to wait another day. An extra gun might come in handy, even if it was in the hands of a relatively raw seventeen year old who was playing it much older.

Spur tied up his mount, left the saddle on and hunkered down on the soft mulch of leafmold under the trees. He leaned against a tree for a time, then stretched out, put his hands under his head and pulled his Stetson down over his eyes blocking out the stars that winked at him through the leaves overhead.

It would be a quick night. He figured they had covered about twenty miles into Indian Territories that day. If the trail kept moving south, he guessed it would end soon. The Jamisons would not want to get much closer to Fort Smith, which sat only a hundred yards from Indian Territories just across the Arkansas river.

A night hawk called but Spur did not hear an answer. Everything seemed natural enough. He would sleep, but the slightest noise out of place within fifty yards would awaken him.

Spur McCoy closed his big right hand around the butt of his Colt .45 and drifted off to sleep.

FOUR

Three men rode up a small valley, then turned into the headwaters of a creek. Each man trailed four horses behind him. Some of the mounts had saddles, others only bridles. All seemed to be riding horses and were broken, trailing quietly. The men agreed on the spot and hid their horses in the brushy woods.

Back at the creek and the shade near a little open spot, they kicked off their boots and splashed in the cool water, then brought out their grub sack.

One man gathered wood for a fire and the others looked over the supplies.

The older one was nearing fifty, with a sun and windburned face, stringy, long hair showing from under a weathered and dirty low-crowned hat. He wore a shirt that was once blue but now was so stained and dirty that color became a mottled blue black. Over the shirt he had a grease spattered leather vest that was never buttoned.

The next man at the food sacks was thirty, with a full beard and bleary eyes. His nose ran and made a mess of his moustache, but he didn't seem to care.

He wiped his sleeve over his nose now and then, watching the older man.

The bearded man wore overalls, with only red long johns showing on top. He had a gunbelt strapped around his waist, and was never far from his rifle, an old Lee.

The younger man came back with wood. He put it down, hollowed out a small spot and began to make a tipi of dry grass. Over the grass he put a second tipi of small dead twigs, then slightly larger ones, until he could cross inch-thick branches over the fragile structure.

He put rocks around the outside of the small fire ring, then struck a stinker sulphur match and pushed it between the larger sticks to the center where he lit the tinder dry grass and small twigs.

The grass flamed up, touched the small twigs that resisted a moment, then burst into flame. From then on it was a gradual warming process as one small stick burned and lit a larger one over it. Soon he had a blazing fire going. He carefully built a square of larger wood around the tipi, then stood back when the older man strode up.

"Finally got a fire going, huh?" the older man said. He pushed the younger one aside. "Damn, you ain't good for nothing, is you, Wort?"

Wort frowned, puzzled, then lifted his brows as he tried to think through the question.

"Not good . . . ?" He grinned. "No sir, Mr. Walton. No sir, I guess not. If you say so."

"Damnit Wort! Keep out of my fucking way! Now stand over there and be quiet."

Wort scowled. "Don't like you swearing at me, Mr. Walton," Wort said, his voice low, nearly an apology.

Walton turned, snorted. "Damn, Wort, don't think I can put up with a crazy like you any longer." He lifted an old Colt .44 from leather and fired once from the hip. The round jolted through Wort's chest, puncturing his right lung, broke a rib and brought a froth of blood to his lips.

Wort stumbled backwarks and sat down, fear and anger on his face.

"Shot me!" he screeched through a mist of blood.

"Damned if I didn't," Walton said.

The third man came running up, his pistol out. He looked at Mort, then back at Walton.

"Hell, Bill, I just couldn't stand the idiot any longer. We just took him on to help with the horses."

"Doctor!" Wort said, his voice losing volume. "Take me to a doctor!" He screeched the last but it ended in a gurgle of blood seeping from his lips.

"Hell, you don't need a doctor, Wort," Bill said. Both the men turned toward him. They glanced at each other, then both lifted their pistols and fired three times each. The rounds ripped the last shreds of life from the mentally retarded man's body, and sprawled him on his back on the rich black soil of the Territories.

"Hell yes, Wort. We'll take your horses to the doctor. You just gave up your third in the string we got!"

Walton chuckled. "Bill, you are bad! Remind me not to get you mad at me."

Bill laughed and motioned toward the food. "Not as long as you feed me good. What the hell we having for chow?"

On a rise thirty yards away through a fringe of trees, a rawhider with a four day's growth of beard stared through a small bush down the slope at the three thieves. He jumped when the shots slammed into the quiet noon time.

He was between fifty and sixty years old. A greasy railroader's bill cap perched on his head hiding dull, dirty gray hair. His face was spotted with sores and he coughed quietly as he watched the killing below.

He had seen the three riders come up the valley, watched them hide the horses and grinned in anticipation. His clothes were so dirty they would stand up by themselves. His name was Spivey and he held the stolen Winchester rifle in his hands like a lover.

Spivey had counted the horses, fifteen! Christ, there was a fortune in horses down there! He could get plenty for them in Fort Smith, no questions asked. The brands might have to be dealt with, but that would be little problem out here.

He reached below him and whacked the girl lying in the grass.

"What the hell you want, old man?" she asked. She rolled over and sat up.

Spivey grinned. She was maybe fourteen, she never had told him. The man's shirt she wore had so many holes in it her breasts both showed through the front. She had a lot to show. Christ, she was built like a brick shithouse! Spivey reached down and grabbed one breast and pulled her up the hill so she could see over the top.

"Right down there is our ticket to Fort Smith. Fifteen horses we can sell. Should mean five, six hundred dollars, we work it right. And I might even buy you some pretties and maybe a new dress."

"Fuck, you better, all the loving sweet pussy I give you even if you is an old bastard." She laughed softly.

Spivey pushed his hand down the front of the shirt and grabbed her breasts and played with them. He rubbed his growing hardon, then scowled.

"First we blast these cruds, then we have a party."

"You promised to save the next young one for me," she said, her dirt caked young face pouting.

"Hell!" He spat into the dirt. "If'n it works out,

girl I'll save you one young prick down there. If'n it works out."

"Good!" she said and tried to snatch his balls. He pushed her hand away.

He let go of her breast and lifted the rifle. One of the targets worked over the fire. Spivey waited until the man was on the side of the fire, then lifted the Winchester and sighted in. When it was just right, he squeezed the trigger. The rifle fired and the heavy round bored through the back of Walton's head and exploded out his right eye, taking half his face with it.

Walton slammed forward, fell full length across the fire and the flames soon licked at his pants legs.

Below in the small camp, the rifle shot was a warning to Bill who dove to the ground, then rolled toward the water where the stream had gouged a two foot deep gully.

"Damn't!" Spivey said. "Only got one."

"Save the other one for me!" the girl whispered, as one hand stroked her breasts.

"Hey! You up there with the rifle." The words came from below in the creek bed.

"Talk up, stranger," Spivey called.

"You got us good. Old Walton, he's cooking on his own fire, dead as a toad. Me, I'd like to live a while. I got me fifteen good horses down here. Split them with you. You get ten, I keep five. Been working two months rounding up these nags. Fair is fair. What do you say?"

"How can we do that?" Spivey called. "I got the rifle, you can't go nowhere." He kept watching but the man did not show himself. Spivey's rifle sight worked over the edge of the cut where the man had vanished. Spivey could kill a fly at a hundred yards with the rifle.

"Hell," Bill called getting some confidence back. "You hold up your rifle by the barrel so I can see it, and I'll go into the woods and take five of the horses and you get the rest. Give me an hour's start and then they are yours."

"Sounds reasonable," Spivey said. "You got a bill of sale for them all, I'd reckon."

Bill laughed. "Hell yes, and I'm the Bishop of New Orleans, too."

Both men laughed at that. Bill lifted up to scan the hill above him, but dropped quickly.

"Well, what do you say?" Bill asked. "Those ten horses should bring you forty dollars a head in Fort Smith."

"You got a deal," Spivey said. He held up the rifle by the barrel.

Below Bill couldn't believe his good luck. He had talked his way right out of getting killed! He eased up a moment, stood, then dropped down out of sight. The rifle stayed high in the air held by the barrel.

"Got to be sure," Bill called. He bent to step up the two feet to the slope and out of the stream bed. As he did he looked down at the ground.

When he looked up again he saw a gaze of blue smoke just as the Winchester fired and felt the slug slam into his shoulder and pitch him backward into the six inches of water in the small creek.

By the time he got to his knees, the Winchester was six feet from him, and the man behind it not the kind to take ten horses when he could have all fifteen. Bill swore and lifted his hands.

"Up here on dry land," Spivey said.

Behind him the girl stood watching. Her skirt had been cut off halfway to her knees, showing delicious curving calves.

Spivey turned to her and motioned.

"Hurry up, we ain't got all day. Fuck him quick and let's get back to the wagon."

She watched Bill. He went to his knees and she saw his shoulder was still bleeding.

"Got to stop the blood draining out of him first," she said. She tore part of his shirt off and made a pad, then pushed it against the wound and told him to hold it there. Then she unbuttoned her shirt and spread back the sides.

Bill stared at her breasts and wailed.

"Them tits of yours are real that are hanging out there?" he asked.

She stepped closer and pushed one breast into his mouth and he moaned as he chewed on it. He remembered what the old man had said.

"Look, girl, I can fuck you good, that what you want. I can stick you where it feels good, any hole you want filled. I got the prick that can do the job five or six times, without stopping. You can ask any of the fancy women in Fort Smith."

"Get on with it!" Spivey shouted. He was collecting the weapons of the three men. So far he had found four six-guns and three rifles.

They all looked up as they heard a wagon coming. It drove up the little valley as far as it could go. An old woman eased down and stared at the pair, then walked up twenty yards to the death scene.

She was a match for the old man, maybe fifty years old, shrunken and thin, with a pinched face as dirty as the others. Her hair was hidden under a sunbonnet. Her breasts had sagged years ago and now hung down almost to her waist, small flopping globs of useless flesh.

She wore a dress that had at one time been a fancy ball dress, but after she had worn it for six months without washing it, the beautiful fabric and its colors had turned into dirt brown and tattered. The skirt drug the ground and was grimy black on the bottom.

She swore at Spivey, then walked over to the man on his knees where he was chewing on the girl's breast. She backhanded the girl across the face, and pushed her away.

"You know it's my turn first around here! This is a young one. Help me undress him."

The girl cringed back for a moment, then with the resiliency of youth smiled and jumped forward tearing at the buttons on his shirt. They stripped his boots off, then pulled down his pants and jerked them off so he was naked.

"Go slow, women! I got enough here for both of you." Bill sat on the grass now, his member stiff and ready. "Lordy, let me see some of them young tits!" he yelped.

The girl opened her shirt and flipped back the sides, then covered herself.

The old woman bent over him, playing with his stiff penis for a minute, then straddled him, lifted her skirts and held him upright as she lowered her crotch squarely on his shaft. She grunted once, then a smile covered her dirt streaked face as she began to bounce up and down on him.

"What the hell you doing old woman? That's no civilized way to fuck! You're an animal. Now big tits over here, yeah. I bet the girl knows how to fuck proper on her back." He wailed.

"Christ, woman, you do know how to get a guy's cock going!" He roared and tried to thrust up as he climaxed, but the woman kept on lifting and dropping.

At last she screeched a bellowing claim of satisfaction and stood up.

She snorted. "Hell's bells, he warn't half good. Look at how fast he shriveled up. Not a stayer. He's all yours, girl. See if you can get him hard again. Bet you can't."

The old woman walked away with a little swagger and went inside the covered wagon.

The girl sat on the grass a dozen feet away from Bill. She had her hands inside her shirt slowly stroking her breasts as she had done as she watched the two coupling. Now she slowly took off the shirt.

She made a little ritual of it, a strip tease, letting him see her pink tipped breasts one moment, covering them, then showing both and covering. Gradually she let one breast show fully, then both and turned to face him.

"Now them is tits!" Bill screeched. He got on his hands and knees and crawled toward her.

"Stay there!" she said. She went down on her hands and knees letting her big breasts hang and sway as she did. She crawled six feet toward him, then rolled on her back and back to her hands and knees making her breasts jiggle.

"God almighty!" Bill breathed. "Them is damned pretty boobs and I want to eat them off you!"

She moved closer but stayed out of reach.

"Sit down," she said. He did and she saw his penis was still not hard.

Slowly she began to stand, then went into a little dance that made her breasts shake and bounce. She worked on the buttons of the long skirt and when it was undone, she began to tease it off her body. It dropped from her waist, lower and lower until pubic hair showed.

Bill moaned and crawled toward her. She scurried away and pulled up the skirt, then bunched it high on her white thighs inching it up and up. Bill screeched in delight and tried to catch her.

By now his penis was stiff and tall and she twirled the skirt away and showed him her back, then she turned slowly until she was facing him and he gasped in wonder and passion.

She walked to him, letting him grab her thighs, then she bent, rubbing her breasts over his face until he caught one and sucked it into his mouth. He was not concerned with the weeks of build-up of dirt and grime on her breast. He sucked and licked and washed it.

When she tired of that she stood, forced him down and stepped over him with her crotch inches from his face.

"Eat it!" she said, her voice husky.

"What?"

"Lick my pussy, stick your tongue up inside me!"

"Goddamn!" He pushed forward and up until his face was buried in the muff of her crotch hair and his tongue worked wonders in a act he had never done before. He tried to move away but her hands caught the back of his head and forced him against her harder and harder until she climaxed and he fell away shaking and laughing.

He grabbed his penis and began pumping it with his hand.

She kicked him in the side.

"No!" she said sharply. She pushed him down with her foot and then fell on top of him and pulled herself up his hard, lean body until they matched and she forced him into her tight vagina.

She screamed as he penetrated and then shrieked in total pleasure as she rode on top of him like a young stallion.

"Christ, woman. Can't you get enough?" Bill exploded after she had climaxed four times. She had stopped him every time he started to drive toward his own satisfaction.

"Twice more," she said and looked over at the old man. She nodded and he lifted his brows in reply. He would do it again! Christ but that made her feel even sexier!

She made it last a long time, working up slowly

and then on the second time she raced fast and hard toward her own climax. She rocked and rolled and surged up and down until he thought she would break him in half.

She surged higher and higher and saw the old man move up beside her. Her passion mounted again and again, then as her face distorted with the surging release of the tremendous pressure she nodded at the rawhider.

Just as she screamed and shivered into a tremendous spasm of fulfillment, the old man lowered a Colt .44 and blasted a round through Bill's forehead.

The girl sensed Bill dying inside her and it pushed her climax to a higher level. She screamed and her whole body went stiff with a sudden paralysis.

Then it was over and she came off him quickly and without looking at his face she began gathering up her clothes. She went over and sat down naked in the small stream and began to wash herself.

"Ain't had a bath in three months," she told the old man. She stood and humped her crotch at him. "I'll get it clean and sweet smelling so you can eat it, too." She laughed and sat down in the water again.

He hardly heard her. He was busy checking the bodies for anything else of value. He had the guns, horses, saddles, and all the paper money and gold coins they owned. There was nothing else.

The old rawhider stood, looking down at the dead, naked man a minute. "Damn fool!" he said. The naked, dead man should have known better than to trust a fucking woman. He should have been thinking how to get away.

The rawhider sat down and watched the young girl in the stream. Look at them tits! Damn it was nice having her along on the trip. They had found her in a wagon after they attacked it just over the line in Arkansas. Her parents had got themselves killed in the fracas. That didn't seem to bother her a lot. She said she didn't like them.

She had been a year younger then, but already she had big tits. The old woman had objected, then realized her man wanted the young body for fucking. That was fine with her. And the young girl could do the cooking and cleaning up, too. It had worked out well.

The first three or four times had been a struggle for both the old man and the old woman to get the girl's clothes off and her legs apart. But after half a dozen times, she realized that she loved to fuck more than anything. After that she had come to him every two days. At his age every two days was about right so he didn't get worn out.

The old rawhider shook his head. Today he couldn't get it up, not even watching her wash herself and teasing him. But tomorrow he would have her again.

Damn, tomorrow would be a day. They would move this string of saddle horses into Fort Smith, and then sell them one at a time over the next two weeks. By the end of that time he would be a rich man!

Christ but she was a pretty woman. He didn't care if she was just fourteen. He rubbed his crotch but nothing happened.

The old rawhider went to look at his new string of horses. What a day tomorrow was going to be!

FIVE

Spur and the bounty hunter Ferrier met back at the dead fire a little after sunup. Spur had the feeling the young man had been waiting for him for some time.

"Figured you for an early riser," Ferrier said.

Spur checked around the fire area. There had been no horses nearby and he found no strange boot-prints.

"Coffee," Spur said.

Ferrier got a fire going while Spur dug into the supplies on his horse and came up with the coffee pot and a jar filled with fresh ground coffee.

By the time the brew was boiling, Ferrier had drawn a rough map on the ground of the Indian Territories, and outlined several spots where he figured the Jamison gang could be holed up.

"All depends if they are new here or if they come back here after every five or six robberies," Ferrier said. "Heard about one gang that had a regular cabin they used. Even hired somebody to stay in it while they was gone so nobody would ruin it or take it over."

Spur sipped the hot black coffee and looked at the map. "We follow the tracks as long as we can. There's a chance we could lose them, but by then we should have some indication which general direction they're headed."

Ferrier nodded. "Fine by me. Not sure I could have read their tracks this far."

Ten minutes later the sky was bright enough to see the hoofprints and they were on the trail. It wasn't poor tracking, rather too many animals that proved their downfall.

Spur quickly found that one additional horse had used the trail since the Jamisons. Two miles farther south two more horses joined the set of prints that showed plainly in the damp places on the trail.

They came to a spot where the faint trail forked. One trail led on down south within spitting distance of the Arkansas border.

Ferrier sat on his horse as Spur got off and tried to read the hoofprints on the packed ground. Now there were eight or ten more sets of marks for him to figure out.

Longjohn Ferrier shook his head. "Don't look like there is much of a chance that the Jamisons would head toward the east. Arkansas is not more than five miles over there, and down another ten or twelve is Fort Smith, state lawmen and the home base for the hanging judge, Mr. Parker. Nosiree. I had my druthers I'd be moving away from Judge Parker."

"That cave you talked about is over that way to the west?" Spur asked.

"That's a fact. Somewhere eight or ten miles. It's possible we could find out something over there." Longjohn stopped. "Damnit no, you look too clean. You'll have to dirty up your clothes and stop shaving for a few days. You got to fit in with the rest of us out here."

Spur kicked at the dust in the road, swung up on his horse and looked at the young bounty hunter.

"Let's try the cave. There are so many tracks right here that I can't even tell if they got this far." Spur rubbed his chin. "How can you travel around out here, being a bounty hunter? Outlaws hate you guys ten times as much as lawmen."

"That's a fact. But they don't know what I do. Had a poster printed up on me. Shows me wanted in Texas, but the reward is only fifty dollars for me as a sneak thief. I use it when I get cornered or need some help. It's a good way to throw them off the track. Just be sure you don't shave any more. Nobody out here shaves."

They rode along the new trail heading east for a mile, then Ferrier pointed off the way to a small stream.

"Let's go down there and we'll get you dirtied up some. Won't be foolproof, but it could get you by."

"Is this absolutely necessary?"

"Only if you want to live a few more days so you can smile as a pretty lady takes off her chemise for you with promises."

"You win."

At the creek Spur took off his shirt and hat and let Ferrier trample them in a muddy shoreline. He wrung out the shirt and the mud smeared it again. The hat he stomped into the mud and water and mashed mud into the brim and crown until it looked unfit to wear.

"Now your face. Get it wet and smear it with dust. Keep at it until it won't wash off. Get some in your hair too, you look too damn much like a federal lawman."

An hour later Ferrier decided Spur McCoy looked as though he had been living in the Territories at least for a few months. He still wasn't dirty enough. What he needed was the kind of grime and greasy dirt that had to be earned, not smeared on.

They got back on the trail and Spur felt gritty and grimy. If he had lived in the same clothes for a month he would have been used to the slow accumulation of dirt. Not this way. He sighed. If it would keep him alive and help him finish his assignment, he could put up with it.

"Tell me about this damn cave," Spur said.

"Only been there once. Guy I was chasing went in and out of there like a shot one night, and I was a day behind him.

"It's a natural cave, a cavern place that some guys say is more than a mile long deep underground. It's got a small stream flowing through it, so water is close at hand, and it's pure too, none of that mineral stuff."

"Men live in there?"

"Damn right. Nobody gets in unless he's vouched for or can outshoot the guard. I gave the guard a twenty dollar gold piece and proved to him I could outdraw him if he got greedy. The man on duty keeps whatever he charges."

"Fires, food, how do the men live?"

"Bring in their food. If somebody gets lucky and kills a deer, they share it. Firewood is carried in, you'll see."

"We can get in?"

"How else can we tell if the Jamisons came this way? When a bunch like them comes past or stays a night, every man Jack of the people inside know it."

"Any women in there?"

"Damn few. I heard there were two whores way up in back by the air shaft, but I never got back there. Guess they could charge whatever they wanted to."

Spur spotted two horsemen riding toward them half a mile ahead. He motioned Longjohn off the trail and they sat on their horses behind some brush as the pair went by. Both were Territories dirty, both looked mean and carried three weapons each.

Spur put his Colt back in leather as the horsemen moved out of sight down the trail.

"Friendly looking pair," he said.

"Friendly ain't important out here," Longjohn said. "Staying alive is the first order of business."

They approached the cave just past midday. The sun was out brightly burning away the morning chill. They had moved into a river valley with a real canyon feel to it. Cliffs sixty feet high rose on both sides of the small shallow stream that seemed to come out of the face of the sheer cliff.

It did.

"This is the underground river I told you about," Longjohn said. "We get to the cave entrance by riding right up the creek. Be sure to duck at the cliff. The opening is just a little higher than a horse's head."

They turned into the water and walked their mounts toward the cliff.

"Let me do most of the talking. Be ready to use that Colt, but don't draw first. We don't want a real shootout."

"I got the idea. Why haven't we seen anyone?"

"This place is like a fort, everyone inside. Duck."

Spur went flat against his mount's neck as the animal walked through the opening in the cliff wall. For a moment it was as black as the inside of a gambler's heart, then his eyes adjusted.

He followed Longjohn who swung to the right to dry ground and eased off his horse.

The cavern sloped up sharply from the small doorway. Sun streamed in lighting the front part. Spur guessed it must be forty feet high ten feet back from the entrance. Beyond that he could see only a few fires burning, and a torch or two.

Somewhere a rough, raucous voice sang a bawdy

song.

"Who the hell are you guys?" a sharp unpleasant voice boomed at them.

"Who the fuck you think?" Longjohn spat back. Then he laughed. "Louie, that you? You still got the door concession? Damn, you must be rich by now."

"Kid, you back so soon?" The voice laughed. "Bet your mommie is chasing you, huh kid?"

"Right, her and a sheriff, Missouri type. We had a misunderstanding about who owned the cash in a general store safe." Both men roared with laughter.

"Longjohn, the bounty on you any higher yet?"

"Nope, still fifty bucks. I keep changing my name so I don't get too valuable. You thinking of turning bounty hunter?"

Spur could see the man now. He sat in a rocking chair beside a formal dining room table. Both were on a wooden floor someone had built. There were two other chairs, and the table was well stocked with whiskey, water and tins of canned meats and at least a few cans of sliced peaches, the cowboy's favorite dessert.

"Who's your ugly friend?"

"Louis, this is Sam Spur, a phony name if I ever heard one. But a hell of a good gun to have on your side. He threw in with me back about ten miles when a damn rawhider decided he liked my horse."

Louis laughed. "Yeah. Rawhiders is for shit, but we got a few. Bad for the neighborhood!" He laughed again. Louis was fat and filthy. Spur guessed he was a short man. Since he was sitting down, rolls of fat flowed around his belt.

"Hey Sam, can you talk?"

"Fer damn sure," Spur said using a slight Texas drawl.

"Oh, shit, another Texan. Hell, five bucks a head to get in. Any argument we shoot out a candle. You win, you get in free. I win, it costs you fifty bucks."

Spur dug out a ten dollar gold piece, an eagle coin, and walked over to Louis. He held it in the palm of his hand, then tossed it in the air. Louis caught it, bit it, then nodded.

"Welcome home. But don't you expect no damn sheets on the beds." Louis laughed. "Hell, don't expect no beds!" His laugh soared into the reaches of the cavern, as Longjohn and Spur walked their horses into the cave.

They passed the first campfire Spur had noticed on the left. Behind it two men lounged on straw mattresses and blankets. They were eating the remainder of a pair of roasted rabbits. The men touched their weapons as Spur and Longjohn walked past.

Around an abrupt turn in the cavern they came to a lighter area, where a thin shaft of light penetrated through a natural chimney opening above.

In the center of the big "room" was a campfire. Horses were picketed around the rim of the oval area that was a hundred feet across. Spur and Longjohn ground tied their mounts against the wall, then moved toward the blaze.

"This is the campfire, the meeting place," Longjohn said. "We should be able to hear anything about Jamisons if they passed or came in."

The fifteen or twenty men around the campfire were all sitting on the rocky floor, resting, talking or just watching the fire. It was a haven for them. If they wanted to talk they talked. Two men played poker in the light of the fire, using gold coins instead of chips. Loaded pistols lay close by each man's hand. It was a warning that to cheat was to die.

Longjohn looked for a familiar face around the circle, at last saw one and moved next to him on the outer ring and sat down.

The man next to them stared at Spur for a moment, then looked at Longjohn and grinned.

"Hi, kid! You make the big time, or you just playing at being an outlaw? Sure as hell hope your hide is worth more than fifty bucks by now."

Longjohn laughed. "Hell no! I ain't gonna tempt any damn part time bounty hunter inside here. Just had a small argument with a sheriff, that's why I came by."

"You two didn't see eye to eye about somebody else's money, I bet," the man said.

"True, true. It was only three hundred, and the damn mercantile had plenty. I only borrowed it for a few years. Damn sheriff was going to put me in the calabose."

"But you shot him?"

"I refused to dicker about such a small amount. I left town."

"And the sheriff came after you."

Spur could see the other man plainly now. He was about thirty, had a full beard and gleaming white teeth. His clothes were not as dirty as some of the others, and he spoke well, as if he was an educated man.

"Johnson, wasn't that the monicker?"

"Not my current one but it will do for now," Johnson said with a laugh.

Longjohn waved at Spur. "My traveling companion, Mr. Sam Spur. Leastwise that's what he said his name was. Handy man in a pistol conversation with a sheriff, though. I can guarantee that."

Spur nodded at Johnson. The other man stared at him for a minute, then bobbed his head once.

"Spur, unusual name," Johnson said.

"It was White last week," Spur said and they all laughed.

Longjohn plunged on. "Least wise I found out why that Missouri sheriff was so nasty. Will Jamison and his boys had relieved the bank of all its paper currency the day before. My timing ain't too good in these matters."

"Jamison again," Johnson said. "Wish he would retire and let the rest of us have a chance. He keeps things all riled up and makes it damn hard for a man on his own."

"I just hoped he hadn't pulled in here and taken over the place," Longjohn said.

"Hell, no chance of that. He's got his own place somewhere, fixed up like a damn fort I hear."

"Heard the same thing," Spur said. He looked at Longjohn. "You said we'd fix some chow in here? We need our own fire?"

"True," Longjohn said. "After we buy some wood." He paused. "Johnson, you got a fire we could rent?"

The man shook his head.

"Hell, come sit by ours then. We'll dig up some grub, too. Don't pay to sit around here by yourself too damn long."

Johnson sat up straighter. "I thank you, young feller. I was starting to feel a mite like bait in somebody's trap. Should be some vacant spots down this drift a ways."

A half hour later they had bought five dollars worth of wood from a man who had a stack, built a fire in a side tunnel and settled down to coffee and slabs of bread and cheese that was just a day from spoiling.

"Glad that damn Jamison ain't coming our way," Longjohn said between sips of the scalding black coffee. "He always brings a new batch of bounty hunters and federal men chasing him."

"He ain't this deep into the Territories," Johnson said. "Hear his place is over near the Arkansas line. That way he gets to his hideout quick and can strike back across the line again."

"No shit?" Longjohn said.

Johnson ate another sandwich and refilled his coffee cup. "One guy who was through here said he stumbled on their place once and it wasn't more than fifteen miles from Fort Smith. Ain't that a belt! And with old Judge Parker just ranting and raving about law and order!"

"Funniest thing I ever heard!" Spur said, faking a laugh that sounded faked even to him.

"Yeah, I figured on him being a hundred miles west of here," Longjohn said.

The voices from farther into the main cave came plainly. Two men were shouting at each other.

A few men began moving past Spur's spot, walking toward the fight. There was no alarm given, no announcement made, but the audience was assembling. Spur, Johnson and Longjohn walked that way. Twenty feet up the cave two fires lit the scene. Two men were facing each other across one of the blazes. Each was bare to the waist. Each held a knife with a six-inch blade. The sharp edges glinted in the firelight.

"You stole it, you sonofabitch!" one man snarled.

"Like hell! It was mine all the time. Come take it away from me you want it so bad."

Those were the last words spoken. The larger of the two men jumped the fire, his knife slashing at the other man who pivoted away and sliced a three inch gash on the attacker's shoulder.

A howl of pain and anger echoed through the cavern.

The smaller man feinted one way, drove in from another angle and sliced the tall man's knife hand.

Now the strategy changed. The big man knew he was outgunned as far as knife fighting skill. He took a big breath, surged one way and then the other to force his target against the wall with no escape, then he drove straight at him, lifted his left arm to take the knife slash he knew was coming from the smaller man.

The blade bit through his arm to the bone.

The wounded man screeched in pain, but rammed against the smaller one with his chest, pinned him against the rocky wall, then drove his knife into the man's side, tugged at it, ripping and slicing forward until the blade came out the smaller man's stomach.

The victor stepped back, watching the man die. He was ripped and sliced to pieces inside, but no vital organs had been touched.

The big man roared in anger, stabbed his bloody knife into the fallen man's groin and slashed at his genitals. Then he bent over the victim who was barely conscious and stabbed his knife into the dying man's eyes one at a time. Screams so agonizingly painful that Spur could scarcely believe they were human bounced off the walls.

With a bellow the big man slashed his knife across the dying man's throat severing both carotid arteries.

He turned, stared at the watchers. Three cuts on his arm and shoulder dripped blood. His knife was blood bathed. He roared and shrieked and charged at the men at the edges of the firelight, then pulled back.

"Leave me alone you sonsofbitches!" he screamed once more and the crowd of watchers began to fade away.

Spur caught Longjohn's elbow.

"Time to go," he said.

Longjohn shivered and nodded.

Back at their fire, they gave it to Johnson, found their horses at the wall of the big room, and led them back toward the front of the cavern.

At the entrance, Louis demanded a complete report on the fight. Spur gave him a brief version of it.

"Just stopped by looking for a friend, but he ain't here," Longjohn said at the door. "So best we be on our way."

"Still to do that candle shooting out?" Spur asked Louis.

"Not a chance, no stakes now."

Spur pulled his horse around, mounted and watched the small fat man. The Secret Agent pulled his .45 and shot the top off a bottle of whiskey sitting on the table beside Louis.

"Just in case you want to know, I'd have beaten your tail off," Spur said. He pushed a new round into the spot just fired and holstered his piece.

Spur touched his hat, moved into the stream and walked his mount to the entrance, leaving his back open to the fat guard if he wanted to try it.

Louis chose the better part of valor and decided to live to fight another day.

Outside, Longjohn stared at Spur in disbelief.

"Christ, you almost ruined the whole thing! Why you have to do that fancy shooting thing? Now he'll remember you and me too. He'll want to know which Fancy Dan outlaw you really are. I won't be able to go back there for a year at least."

Spur grinned. "I had a bad day. There I was rubbing shoulders with a hundred outlaws, and I couldn't even arrest one of them. It was the most frustrating few hours of my life. What did you expect me to do, play poker with those cutthroats?"

Longjohn lifted his brows. "Hey, I never thought of it that way. I guess it was tough for you. Where we heading?"

"Back the other way, east again, back toward the Arkansas line. I want to see where the other fork in that road goes."

"I'm with you. Maybe now that we have it narrowed down a little we should split up so we can cover more ground quickly."

Spur thought about it as they rode. It was a good idea. By the time they got to the fork in the trail it was late in the afternoon. They could camp together one more night, then lay out the territory to cover and arrange a meeting place for each day at sundown. Spur nodded and they looked for a good place to conceal themselves for the night.

SIX

Will Jamison and his band approached their hideaway cabin the way they always did when all of them had been away. They came at it on foot from four different directions. They moved slowly, stalking it, rushing quietly from one bit of protection to the next as they came up on the small building.

Unless one knew exactly what to look for, the cabin itself was extremely hard to see.

Will moved twenty feet and stopped, every nerve in his body alert to danger. Someone could have found the place and taken it over while they were gone.

He moved again and could see the shape of the door through the branches and vines that covered the structure. His breath came quickly now as he watched the place.

Will saw no movement, no sign that anyone had been there since they left. No smoke came from the stone chimney. They never came to the cabin in the same way so no trail could be established.

A mockingbird chattered a shrill cry and Will

made the same sound back at it. The call meant Phil had seen nothing unusual.

He heard one more call on the far side, then Dale broke from behind a tree and raced to the cabin door and jolted it open, a pistol in each hand.

He vanished inside and a moment later was back, hogslegs leathered and he waved.

"All clear, come on in," he said and went back inside.

Will came from behind the tree and moved forward. They had looked a long time before they found this place. It had been built maybe forty years ago, and the brush and small trees of the Brushy Mountains had grown over and aroud the place until it blended in perfectly with its surroundings. They did a little work to make it even harder to spot.

They put in new windows, hung a solid strong door and dug an escape tunnel out the far side that exited ten feet the other side of the wall. It had been home to the Jamison gang now for almost two years.

As far as Will knew, nobody had ever found the place, at least not while they had been there.

The Brushy Mountains were an ideal spot for them to hide. The growth reminded Will of the Big Thicket country in Texas. The brush and vines were so thick that no man in his right mind would try to plow through it without some kind of a trail.

A native to the area could get lost in five minutes, and would need half the morning to find his way out. Only two trails crossed the area anywhere near their cabin.

They had built a small pole corral in a little canyon half a mile away, and kept their horses and spares there. They had worked out several general routes to get to the cabin from the corral. None was exactly a trail, and in spots they crawled under the thick brush rather than through it. The difficulty of the entrance was what gave them such good protection.

Will walked into the cabin and saw that Phil had a lamp lit and was laying a fire in the stove. They made it a habit never to light a fire in the stove or the stone fireplace until after dark. It made tracking the smoke damned near impossible through the thicket at night.

Will tossed his saddlebags on the table and the sack of currency.

"Counting time, boys," he said. His sons and Mat Rorick grinned and gathered around the two sacks.

As usual, Will did the counting and dividing. He was the boss. He laid out the wrapped bundles of bills according to denomination. He stacked the loose bills the same way for counting later. There was one bundle of fifty dollar bills and one of hundreds.

None of the men had ever seen a hundred dollar bill before. Will put them aside and concentrated on the rest. When he had it all laid out, he began dividing it into four piles.

The expressions on the men's faces grew as the stack he had claimed as "his" grew and grew.

"Must be forty thousand here!" Will said. "Damn, one of the biggest hauls we've ever made. One more like this and I can go back to New York City and live like a king for the rest of my days."

Dale grinned. "I think I'll keep Milly in Fort Smith instead of her going back and forth to Missouri at the time. Hell, we could buy that house we been using! But I ain't ready to quit yet. Nosiree bob. Got me a lot more banks to do!"

Will preened his drooping moustache and stared at his oldest. "Don't push it too far, boy. We been damn lucky up to here. We kept things under control. But it can't last. One of these days the surprises will all be against us, and some of us could get killed.''

"Like Gabe," Rorick said.

"Yeah, like Gabe. He was hurt bad and we couldn't help him none riding on a horse.''

"Pa, would you have finished me off that way if it had been me gut shot back there?" Phil asked.

Will Jamison looked at his youngest son and shook his head. "Don't rightly know, Phil. Hell no! I'd have brought you back, nursed you myself. Gabe, he never fit in with the family all that well. Not like Rorick here does.''

By the time the money was divided they each had a little over ten thousand dollars.

"Christ, a cowboy would work for thirty years to make this much money!" Dale said. "We made it in a day and a half!" He jumped up and danced a little jig on the hard packed earth floor.

Will laced his fingers together in back of his head and leaned back on the box he sat on by the table.

"Yeah, right. So maybe we should just hang up the iron and enjoy our money. Sure is sounding better to me all the time.''

"But you're old, Pa. You got to be over forty now!''

"Ain't exactly in the grave yet, boy!''

"Didn't mean it that way. Hell, I'm only twenty-two. I figure I'm just getting started.''

"You found a good woman yet, Phil?''

"Hell no. When I got time to meet a nice woman? I just barely got time to fuck a whore now and then.''

Phil left the table and went to the corner where his bunk stood against the log wall. He moved the bunk out and scraped an inch of dirt away from the floor until he uncovered the top of a sturdy metal box. He wiped away all the dust and dirt from the top, then swung it up.

The rest of them ignored him as if he wasn't there. He looked down at the stacks of bank notes.

"God damn!" he said softly. On a scrap of paper he had written a figure. It said $38,325. He laid the new money in the hole, put the loose bills that amounted to $187 in his pocket and then made a note on the total. He added the two figures and grinned. He had a total of $48,854!

Phil put the top down softly, spread the dirt over the spot and pounded it down hard with a board, then stepped on the board to make sure. He swung his bunk back in place and dusted off his hands.

Will pointed at the fire and Dale lit a match to the paper and kindling. Dale was their chief cook.

Will had spread out a game of solitaire on the rough wood table top. He glanced up at Phil.

"You still don't trust banks, do you, Phil?"

"Hell no. I seen too many of them go busted." He chuckled. "Hell, I made about thirty of them go bust!"

"How much do you have salted away down there now in that box?"

"Why you wanta know?"

"It's a mighty big temptation."

"How? Nobody but us know it's there!"

"How much, Phil?"

Phil wrote a figure on a piece of paper and handed it to his father. Will read it and pushed it in the small cast iron stove.

"Too damn much, Phil. I got my cash in a bank. I dress up and shave and wash and everything when I go in there as Marshal Jones. In that town I am Marshal Jones. I could ride in there tomorrow and buy a house, go to church and start breeding me some race horses."

"If the bank don't go bust."

"Yeah, that's right."

They didn't talk about the fortune under Phil's bunk again.

"Hell, me, I'm gonna buy myself a big saloon," Dale said. "Have about thirty gambling tables, and a long bar and big goddamn mirrors, and maybe about six fancy women upstairs!" He nodded. "Shit! I got enough money now to buy the best saloon in almost any town I want. Maybe one of the bigger cow towns where there's lots of money floating around. Or maybe one of them fancy-schmantzy places in Houston!"

"Quit dreaming and cook our supper," Rorick said, grinning. "You want any help? I'm starved half to death."

"Sure, peel the potatoes," Dale said. Rorick was almost like family, had been with them since their second bank job. "Rorick, what the hell you gonna do with all your money?" Dale asked.

"Me? Told you. Gonna head out for Wyoming and buy myself a spread and get the best beef breeding stock I can buy, and go into the cattle business. Intend to have me five thousand beef on the hoof by the end of three years."

Phil laughed. "Damn, you must flat out like to work. You ever been a cowboy? You get rained on and step in cow shit and sleep on the damn hard ground and have beans and salt pork to eat a dozen days in a row. I never worked so hard in my life as I did on that damn cattle drive to Kansas."

"I'll be the boss," Rorick said. "I got me enough money to sit back and drink good whiskey and pay somebody to do the dirty work."

Will went outside and checked the exterior of the cabin. It was just as it had been. Vines and young trees had grown up around it giving it a natural camouflage. The roof had long since picked up enough leafmold to sprout grass, and now a heavy grass thatch covered the old roof, helping make it warmer and more waterproof.

The cabin had been built backed up against a twenty foot sheer rock wall. Nobody could get behind it. The front and sides could be defended, and shooting holes had been built in to give complete protection all three ways. The windows were small and high up so a man would have a struggle coming through them. The door had a pair of oak two by fours that dropped in half-inch thick iron straps to bar the outward opening door.

Safe as a babe in his crib.

Will went back inside. He could smell the fried potatoes and onions now. They had brought fresh provisions with them, picking them up at the general store just before they hit the bank up in Willow Creek. He was hungry enough to eat half of Texas.

Will looked toward the trail that ran a half mile from them through brush. He heard nothing. Will Jamison grinned. Just goes to prove what a man can do when he plans ahead. But a man has to plan everything. Even the end of the game. He was thinking about that more and more.

He had meant what he said about being lucky. Their luck could not hold. They had lost only two men, killed in thirty-seven bank robberies. It simply couldn't last.

Will shrugged and went in when Dale called that it was suppertime.

The next morning Phil and Mat Rorick lounged in a shady spot outside the cabin. Rorick heard it first. He sat up and stared into the brush. Phil caught the sound and reached for his rifle.

Rorick caught up his from beside the door and without a word they faded toward the sound. They had no idea who or what the sound might be, but it was too close to the cabin to be ignored.

They glided through the dense brush and woods without a sound. Both had learned to be expert woodsmen, and now they put that to good use. They looked at each other, made signs and split twenty yards apart. They paused, listened, caught the sound again and moved angling to the right.

Phil watched the brush and woods ahead. In a small open space he saw nothing and moved without a sound to a large shortleaf pine. He edged around it staring ahead.

Out of the corner of his eye he saw Rorick move up and pause. They both waited. The sounds came again this time to the left. They moved that way keeping their twenty yards separation.

Phil wormed his way through a tangle of sycamore, gum and hickory trees, then paused beside a huge oak.

Rorick was slightly ahead of him.

He caught movement in front. Phil concentrated on the scene then picked out the movement near a gum tree. An Indian crouched there, bow and arrow in his right hand, three more arrows in his left. He seemed to be naked, but Phil guessed he had on a loincloth.

It was the first Indian Phil had seen this close to the cabin. Phil would make short work of him. He lifted his rifle, then looked at Rorick. The other man held up his hand in a wait signal and pointed to his right.

Before Phil could sight in on the Indian, a four point buck deer wandered from behind a screen of brush and grazed directly in front of Rorick, no more than thirty feet away.

They looked at each other, both nodded and each aimed at the closest prey.

Phil and Rorick fired almost at the same time. Phil saw the Indian move just as he shot. The native stood, and started to draw his arrow. The round slammed into his right leg. The Indian bellowed in pain, then limped around the tree out of sight.

Phil looked at the deer. It was hit, but it bounded away to the right.

"Let's get them both!" Phil shouted. He chased his Indian and Rorick went after the wounded deer.

Phil knew the Indian was still armed. An arrow through the chest could be as deadly as a .45 slug. He ran from cover to cover, then darted across an open spot. An arrow whispered as it cut the air just to his right. He dove to the ground, rolled and came up behind a tree.

Ahead he saw only a big oak tree which the Indian probably stood behind when he shot. The redskin was gone. Phil jumped up and ran for the tree, made it and checked around the base in the grass and leaves. He found splotches of blood.

"Bleeding like a stuck hog!" Phil said softly, then moved ahead, watching both ways, pausing and listening.

Soft sounds came from directly ahead. Indian walk! He moved silently for ten feet. The brushy area opened and Phil ran forward as fast as he could, the rifle at port arms but ready to fire.

He saw the Indian through the light timber, brought up his Springfield .45 army rifle and fired. He saw the slug hit the Indian in the shoulder and slam him down.

Phil ran forward, but used the protection of the foot-thick shortleaf pine when he stopped to watch. He could see one leg of the Indian sticking beyond a big tree.

Phil paused, then jolted ahead again. He was in an open space twenty feet from the redskin when the brave sat up and fired an arrow at Phil. The shaft caught him in the side, sliced through his shirt and nipped a half inch of skin then tangled in his shirt and hung there.

Phil stopped, looked down at his side, then roared in anger. His long rifle came up just before the Indian could loose another arrow. Phil's shot caught the Brave just under the chin and drove down through his neck and ruptured four discs in his spinal column and snuffed his life out in an instant.

Phil left the arrow where it hung in his shirt and eased up to the savage. He wore a loincloth and a headband. Phil kicked him but saw that he was dead, so he bent over and pulled the bow from the death grip and picked up the two arrows he had dropped. The bow was short but effective. He took them with him.

It took Phil ten minutes to find Rorick after he heard a second and then third rifle shot to the right.

If the buck had been lung shot it could run a half mile before it died. Rorick must have stopped it sooner than that.

Phil found Rorick in high spirits. He had just cut the deer's throat and hung it on a stub branch low on a pine tree to let the animal bleed out.

"Got the sucker!" Rorick shouted. "Damn are we going to eat tonight! Liver and brains! Tongue sandwich and then all the venison steaks we can hold. If we can find enough sun I want to slice some of that venison thin and try to dry it, you know, like the Indians do."

He looked up. "You got an arrow sticking in your side!"

Phil laughed. "Near miss. That's one fucking redskin who ain't gonna bother us no more. Let's clean that critter there and cut him in half and I'll help you carry it back to the cabin."

When they struggled to the hideout with the venison, they were met with aimed rifles.

"Heard the shooting and didn't know what the hell was going on," Will said. "Next time you go hunting, you goddamned well better tell me about it. I might have blasted both of you!"

"Sorry, Pa. Happened all sudden. Caught a damn injun stalking this buck, so we stalked them both!"

"Yeah, all right. For venison steaks for dinner I'll forgive you."

Dale was already examining the carcass. He took out the liver and then hung the halves at the side of the cabin. He cut off steaks and took it all into the cabin to start a smokeless fire. Will had just given him permission for a noontime fire, unusual, but he wasn't going to argue.

Rorick stuffed his hands in his pockets and walked up to the other man.

"Will, I been wondering if I could take off for town. I'm getting hornier than an old he-goat."

"Want to spend some money, right? Hell, I don't know. Let's eat first, then we'll decide. I'm still mad as hell about all that shooting so close to the cabin. That venison helps, though!"

The fried liver and onions and venison steaks put them all in a good mood. Phil counted his money again, Rorick decided to have a long nap in the shade, and Will contemplated his future. Rorick figured he'd get a good night's sleep and build up his strength for another day.

Besides, Rorick wanted to stay and eat as much of the venison as he could hold. He got up from his nap, carved out some big steaks from the buck and began slicing them into thin strips half an inch wide and a foot long. He'd heard the thinner the better.

When he had twenty of them done he hung them on a rack he had made with sharpened pointed sticks. He set the rack in the sun and used a pine branch to scare the flies away. After a half hour he got tired and took another nap.

The flies returned, the sun started drying out the venison which might someday become jerky.

Will leaned back in the chair he had taken outside and thought about where he wanted to settle down. His wife had died in an epidemic of smallpox ten years ago. Now with money he could go anywhere he wanted to.

Before he decided he fell asleep.

SEVEN

McCoy and the bounty hunter, Longjohn Ferrier, split up at dawn that morning. Ferrier went farther south to check out some hideouts he knew of where the Jamison gang might be. The Secret Agent worked back toward the fork in the road where he first lost the Jamison gang's tracks. He wanted to try the other fork in the hope that he could pick up the quartet's prints again.

The spot he sought was farther than he remembered. He met no one on the trail and when he came to the fork he moved down it a quarter of a mile before he got down and checked the ground.

Here and there he could still find evidence of the four horses. Most of the prints were leading the other way, toward the interior.

Spur checked for sure, then began walking the ground, checking out the prints every ten yards. They continued. Three miles later they were still showing.

Around a bend in the trail, Spur stopped quickly. In a small side valley he saw a wagon being driven by an old woman. A young girl on horseback led a string of ten or twelve mounts. The little caravan came out of the valley onto the trail heading toward Spur.

He jolted into the woods until he was out of sight and listened for the group to go by. The girl's voice came suddenly through the woods as she shrilled at the old woman. Then she laughed as the older woman screamed in rage and swore at her for as long as Spur could hear them. Sounded like a friendly country family. When he was sure they were out of sight, Spur went back to the trail and worked south. A half mile on he found a change. Spur studied the tracks for ten minutes before he figured it out. There were only three set of prints. Why?

He moved down a quarter of a mile and studied the narrow trail once more. Now there were only two sets of hoofprints in the ground. They showed plainly in the soft spot where a spring wet the trail for fifteen yards.

The riders were leaving the trail one at a time. It could be that they were near their hideout so they didn't want to wear a trail to it. They went through the woods, a different way each time to prevent pounding a trail. Which side had they ridden away on? Spur backtracked until he found three sets of prints he was sure belonged to the same horses.

Then he moved forward until he spotted the spot the third horse left the main trail. It moved to the left. Spur studied the country. The main north-south trail wound along the edge of the low rim of hills. They were called the Brushy Mountains he'd noticed on his map. The hills were covered with shortleaf pine and a million hardwood trees. Around, through and between the trees lay a mass of low growing, hedge-thick brush.

He'd seen spots like that before that you couldn't cut through with a team and a mowing machine.

All he had to do was follow the tracks to the

hideout. Spur frowned. It should not be that simple. He guessed he was in for some surprises.

Tracking the lone horse through the dense woods was easier than Spur had figured. A hundred years of leafmold on the forest floor meant the horse left deep gouges in the six inches of dead leaves, pine needles, molding leaves and newly formed soil.

The trail led through sparse pine, around a dense thicket Spur could not even see through, back near the main trail, then turned dead into the mountains and went up a small ravine, over the top, around more thickets and into a heavily timbered section of hardwoods: oaks, hickory, elms and sycamore.

Spur battled his way through low hanging branches as he followed the trail. Anyone who went to this much trouble to hide his camp had to be an outlaw. The gang members had to do this each time they left or entered the hideout.

Ten minutes later he had followed the tracks to a small open place. He figured it to be a quarter of a mile across. He could see the tracks starting through the center of the meadow. He paused in the heavy brush. Should he show himself and follow the tracks? Or should he stay under cover of the brush and ride around the edge of the opening, and find the tracks on the other side?

It would take longer to go around.

Spur shrugged. There was no choice. He had to go around and stay hidden. He worked as quickly around the meadow as he could, but found heavy brush again and had to detour. He figured it took him almost an hour to move a mile.

When Spur came to the middle of the valley on the far end, he picked up the tracks easily as they left the meadow. The woods were more open here and for a moment he thought he smelled wood smoke. After being in the open for a few days, he could pick up the scent of wood smoke five miles downwind from a small campfire.

But this time he was not sure. It could have come from a fire a dozen miles away and carried here, settling in a spot with little wind.

He moved on.

Spur came out on the edge of a small cleared space no more than thirty yards across. It looked as if it had been a small lake at one time. Now it held only swaying green grass. His horse reached down for a mouthful. As Spur pulled up her head he saw a horseman ride into the opening directly across from him, and then another man behind him.

Both men looked up, startled.

Spur jerked his mount to the side, driving her back into the deeper woods.

Two pistols cracked almost at once as the men fired. They were out of range for anything but a lucky lofted shot. Spur got deeper into the woods and listened. The others were pounding across the dry lake bed directly toward him.

Now he was the hunted, not the hunter!

In the second and a half it had taken Spur to see the two riders and react, he noticed that both wore full beards and rode dark horses. That was all he remembered.

He paused now, checking his escape routes. The two men could be in the Jamison gang, maybe heading out to town or another camp site. He had blundered into them. Now he had to stay alive.

He charged through the most open spot of woods he could find, cut around a thicket and moved generally east. He would touch the main trail south sooner or later.

A rifle slug whined over his head and he jerked the horse to the left behind another heavy growth of thicket. He could try for an ambush, but these two would follow his prints and sniff it out. Maybe,

maybe not. It was worth a try when the right spot showed itself.

Spur charged ahead like a man running for his life. He smashed through light brush he usually would go around, he slithered down a ravine and bulled up the other side. Then just over the small ridgeline he brought the blowing horse to a stop, slid off and jerked the Spencer from the boot.

He bellied up to the top of the little ridge just as the first rider showed on the far side. Spur sighted in on the lead man and was about to fire when he jerked the horse downhill and rode hard. Spur didn't have a chance at the second man who cut through some timber and angled toward his leader. Spur decided he would hold off on his ambush until he could nail one of them and not just warn them.

He rode hard again, passed a small Indian camp, but saw it was a temporary affair. There was nothing there to offer protection or ambush potential.

He continued downhill working toward the trail. Spur had no idea how far from it he might be. Then he remembered that the survivors in Willow Creek said the Jamison gang had the best and fastest horses they had ever seen.

What he had to do was turn this surprise into an advantage. They had no idea who he was. So why shoot? They probably shot at anyone who got close to their cabin. So he must have been close to their hideout.

Spur turned back away from the trail, found a small rise with an open area in front of it and tied his horse to a tree, then slithered up to the top of the rise.

They charged into the opening, cut back to the trees, but not before Spur put two rifle rounds after them. He had no chance to aim, and at two hundred yards it was a chancy shot. At least he had tried. It would slow down their tracking.

He got back on his mount and circled back the way he had come, hoping he was moving toward their hideout again. That might make them furious, and force them into a mistake.

He rode for ten minutes then stopped in some heavy brush and waited and listened. He heard nothing for five minutes, then far behind he heard a horse snort and blow before a hand quickly gripped the muzzle.

They were coming. Spur scowled. He needed something special, unusual that they wouldn't expect. He looked around the woodsy area. Lots of brush, spots of thicket and a few big pine trees.

Pine trees!

Yes! He spurred his horse forward until he found a good one, then rode the animal fifty yards to the side out of sight. He took the Spencer rifle and hurried back to the tree. Spur slung the Spencer over his back by the sling, then using the convenient hand holds the lower dead branches made, he climbed.

When he was thirty feet up the looked for a good perch. Ten feet higher he found it, three four inch thick limbs that came out of the trunk within a few inches of each other. They made a good platform for him to sit on.

There was enough new growth of needles to completely hide him from below. He moved several small branches until he could see his back trail, then he settled down to wait.

Within a few minutes he heard them coming, then saw the first one round a big pine and pause. They were two hundred yards away. Spur waited. They came closer and the next time he had an open shot, he aimed, sighted in carefully and fired.

The round went over the man's head. Spur berated

himself. How often had he told troops that when you're high and shooting down on someone, the round often carries high?

At the crack of the rifle, both the men on horses jerked the animals into the heavy brush and big trees concealing and protecting them. He sent two more rounds through the brush but there was no chance to hit the men.

Spur waited five minutes, then realized the pair had known their position and retreated prudently. The big trees masked their withdrawal and he had no shot.

McCoy climbed down the tree, ran for his horse and kept moving. He was sure they would circle his position to pick up his tracks.

He had no mind to keep running. It was not his style. He would rather stand and fight any day, but it would be on his own terms. If he picked time and place he would have the advantage. He watched his back trail now more frequently.

Backtracking! Yes, he should have thought of it before. He was in a fairly open woods now and sent the mare at a gallop for a quarter of a mile. Then he hid her in some brush, took the Spencer and hurried back along his own trail. He would move up on them, knowing they would be coming along his tracks like a steam engine.

What he needed was a good firing position. A spot where he could do a proper ambush, be safe and at the same time have a marked advantage.

He found it fifty feet ahead. A pine tree had grown tall, but it split when it was small into two trunks. Now the tree was four feet wide at the base, and eye high off the ground the trunks went their separate ways, leaving a perfect "V" slot for firing.

Spur rested the Spencer in the slot. He could sight down the barrel when standing flat-footed behind the tree. He had perfect cover and concealment except for six inches of his head. That would be a tough target. All he wanted was one good, clean shot.

As he waited he saw that the sun had passed its zenith. It could be a little after one in the afternoon. The sun would set around five o'clock. He had four and a half hours of daylight left.

Ten minutes later he heard them coming. Both men were mounted, reading the trail, picking up the pace where the brush thinned. The man in front held up his hand and stopped. He listened for a moment, shook his head and they moved foward. They vanished into a small dip, then came up and directly toward him only sixty yards away.

Spur sighed on the man's chest as the target rode forward. Spur knew the man had a beard from the time he had seen him up close before. He remembered the people in Willow Creek said two of the robbers had full beards and two were clean shaven except for drooping moustaches.

Spur refined his sight, tracked the target past a patch of brush, then had a clean shot. He squeezed the trigger.

On the lead horse, Matthew Rorick seemed to sense the shot. He looked straight ahead at the split tree, started to raise one hand, then the heavy .52 caliber round smashed into his chest, tore through his heart and exploded out his back splattering Phil Jamison with his friend's blood.

Rorick slammed off his horse and onto the ground. His arms flew wide, he hit on his head and shoulders, then tumbled over on his back, his eyes staring straight upward.

Phil Jamison seemed frozen in place for a fraction of a second, then he screamed, jerked his mount to the side and charged through the brush and out of sight.

Spur put three more rounds into the brush where

the man had vanished, then he lifted up and watched the whole area. He saw movement through the brush and fired again, but heard no cry.

Now the hunted became the hunter again.

Spur waited ten minutes, than ran and got his horse and rode up to the spot where the body lay. He checked the surrounding area, found only the trail of one horse moving away quickly. He went back to the body and checked it for identification. Spur found one letter addressed to Matthew Rorick. The name clicked.

Rorick was listed as one of the non-family members of the Jamsion gang. The body held no other personal items.

Rorick's horse munched grass a dozen yards away. Someone would find her eventually.

Spur took the nearly new Henry repeating rifle from the boot and a .45 caliber pistol from the dead man, mounted up and began tracking the survivor.

In the back of his mind, Spur was hoping that the other member of the Jamison gang would ride straight back to the hideout. After a half hour of tracking, Spur realized the man ahead of him was too smart to run right home. He was a tracker, too, and knew that such a move would endanger the rest of the clan.

The man would try to even the score, to put Rorick's killer down. Spur began to watch for an ambush. He changed directions suddenly every two or three minutes, moving ahead but hoping to confuse a sniper.

The prints in the soft footing showed that the rider was making fast time whenever possible. Spur discarded his elusive tactics and pressed foward faster. It was plain now that the rider was heading due west, away from the border, and perhaps away from his hideout. That was a natural move.

Twenty minutes later, Spur came to the north-south trail and figured that the man he was chasing had turned his mount south. The lawman had guessed the rider would go the other way. Now the chances for an ambush were greater. There was room for an open shot from the brush at almost any point along the wide open trail.

Spur had no choice. He had to ride the trail, he had to move slowly and track.

Again he tried fast tracking. He rode a hundred yards at a jump, checked for the prints, when he found them he rode fast another hundred and searched.

The sun was just touching the tops of the Brushy Mountains on his left with the last rays of the day, when Spur came to a large meadow with patches of hardwoods sprinkled through it. The beaten trail cut through the left of the open place.

Spur saw with surprise that the tracks of his man veered to the right and angled for a patch of oaks and hickory trees two hundred yards away. Spur rode quickly back into the woods for protection, then he studied the meadow.

A small stream issued from the woodlands, and cut across the meadow. In times of flash floods, the small stream must be a roaring torrent, because it had dug a channel eight feet deep through the meadow. The wandering stream came to within fifty feet of the first batch of woods out in the flat space where the rider had headed.

Spur figured the stream would be shallow. He rode into the hock deep water and hunkered down to be out of sight of the oak woods, then turned downstream and walked his horse quietly until he could see the target batch of trees.

He came out of the stream on a sloping bank and galloped flat out for the treeline. A rifle spoke once, then again, but Spur had dodged his mount and the lead missed. By then he was in the cover.

The shots had come from his left.

Spur rode forward slowly, watching every direction, listening for the smallest sound that was out of place. He heard nothing. He saw no one. Remembering his tree climb, he checked the oak trees as he moved, but found no sniper.

Now he had a time deadline. If he could not find the other man before darkness, the game would be over. The enemy could slip away in the night, then lay a confusing, impossible to follow trail and vanish.

The man had to be a Jamison. There were only the three of them left in the gang now. If this Jamison got away, it would be ten times as hard to sneak up on their hideout and take them.

No matter how slowly Spur rode, the horsehooves made noise in the dry leaves and twigs. Spur was at the point of leaving the mount and walking when he smelled a foreign element. A moment later he knew what it was.

Smoke!

He looked behind him and saw the smoke trails. A fresh fire billowed to his right and then he saw torches thrown directly in front of him and to the side. They had set on fire the dry grass and ten years of dry leaves and gushed up into a fierce fire before he had time to ride forward.

The horse reared. He pressed toward the right side where there was no fire. Before he got there, the wind whipped a sheet of flames over the escape route and he was surrounded!

Spur sat on the horse holding the frightened animal in check. The fire directly ahead blew at him on a strong wind and came at a surprising speed. There was no chance to ride through the fire on either side.

He began backing away from the flames, then he turned the mare and walked back with the wind toward where the fire burned behind him.

Spur knew he had only one chance of getting out of the firestorm circle alive. He had helped fight a fire in Colorado one summer. They used to do what they called backfiring. For this they would go in front of a roaring fire and do a controlled burn in the path of the flames.

They would backfire it, so when the raging, out of control, firestorm came to the burned area, it would have nothing else to burn and would go out.

Spur stared at the flames behind him. The wind whipped them away from him toward the edge of the grove. On the upwind side was a growing black and smoking ribbon of fire free land! It expanded slowly as the sudden flames burned the ground cover and some small brush, but they were not hot enough to set the larger trees on fire.

Spur checked behind him again, fighting the smoke that swept in on him. The fire was twenty yards away and moving quickly. He urged the mare forward. She refused to step onto the charred ground. Spur jumped off, grabbed the reins, then tied his kerchief over the horse's eyes and led her gently into the blackened, still smoking remains of the backfire. Smoke still drifted up, but it was better than the flaming alternative just behind him.

The horse moved obediently, then shied to one side as her foot hit a hot spot. She walked forward again and Spur came close to the flaming brush on the up wind side of the fire as it burned closer to the edge of the woods.

When he stopped he was fifty feet from the raging flames behind him blowing on the wind. It would burn itself out in another ten feet. He nodded slowly, lifted into the saddle and moved toward the edge of the woodland which had burned through to the grass as the flames died out. Only a few tendrils of smoke remained.

He took the blindfold off the mare, kicked her in the flanks and galloped the last dozen yards, broke through a smoldering section of dry grass into the open meadow where the green grass resisted the flames.

Spur lifted the Spencer from the boot and made sure the safety was off, then began circling the fire blackened island of trees. He found no one. It took him a second circle moving slowly to discover the tracks.

They were fresh and showed that one horse had galloped north toward the trail.

One Jamison had escaped. He would soon be back with the rest of the family in the gang's hideout. Spur didn't have a prayer of catching him now, or tracking him in the darkness. He would report Rorick's death and warn them that someone was hot on their trail.

As Spur rode back to the track he turned off just before the sun went down and found a thicket where he could sleep in comparative peace and safety.

Tomorrow he would return to the trail and move toward the Jamison's hideout. Now he was certain that it was somewhere south of where he had been surprised by the pair of gang members. He would have little trouble finding that spot again, he was sure of that.

But from there on it would be much harder to get to the hideout, especially with the Jamison's expecting him to be coming and waiting for him with all rifles loaded and ready and held by itchy trigger fingers.

EIGHT

Coffee boiled in the small pot sitting on the side of the coals of the dawn fire Spur had built. It was a small fire so it would not attract any attention. He had moved from the thicket to a fairly well protected brushy spot near a chattering creek. Coffee would take care of his breakfast.

Spur thought ahead, remembering where he had been when the two gang members had stumbled on him. He would be able to find that little meadow again, he was sure.

He lifted the tin coffee cup, drained it and was about to stand when the serene morning quiet was shattered with a rifle shot and his coffee pot slammed off the fire as a heavy slug tore into it and knocked it a dozen feet into the brush.

Spur's right hand darted to his holster but a voice stopped him.

"Sonny, you touch that iron and the next slug goes through your chest. You aimin' to die young?"

Spur turned his head slowly, his hand frozen against the butt of his Colt .45.

Twenty feet away three rifles aimed at him over

the top of a fallen log. Spur let out a long held breath and slowly lifted his hands over his head.

"Damn smart!" an old woman's voice croaked.

"This one is all mine," a younger woman said, her voice surging into a wailing high laugh.

They stood one at a time, the old man first. He was in his fifties, rawhider dirty, unshaven, matted hair, an ugly high-crowned hat and below the rim, beady eyes that took in Spur's rig, horse, fire and sack of grub.

The younger woman stood. Spur had no idea how old she was, under wenty, dirty blonde hair in strings around her face and shoulders. The man's shirt she wore had been cut off at her waist and had holes and tears in it. Through one of the holes a tanned breast peaked showing all of the softly pink areola. She didn't notice or didn't care.

"Cover him!" she said and moved forward like a wild creature, ready to jump away at any time. She went to the side, careful not to get between the rifle and Spur, came up behind him and slid the six-gun from his holster.

"Check for a hideout," the old man said.

She did, from the back, her hands feeling his chest, his arms, and torso, then she came up each leg, took a knife from the boot sheat, then patted around his crotch more than was needed.

"Can't find nothing else," the girl said.

The old woman stood, cackling. Her face was drawn, wrinkled, worn out. She laughed again. "If'n you can't find nothing else at his crotch, you don't know where to look!" She roared again, slapping her thigh. Her fancy dress had seen better nights. Now it was filthy and showed how her shrunken breasts sagged almost to her waist.

The girl stepped back, looking at Spur.

"He's a pretty one, ain't he?"

"Mine," the old woman said.

"You got the last one first!" the girl screamed. "My turn. Fair is fair!"

"Ain't no such thing as fair, girl," the old man said. He walked up to Spur and stared up at him. Spur was nearly a foot taller than the slender rawhider.

Suddenly the man's right fist jolted out and crashed into Spur's jaw. The move was so quick and such a surprise that Spur staggered backward.

The old man punched Spur twice in the belly and another shot at his jaw before Spur caught his hands and held them.

"Let go!" the old man screamed. "Let go or I'll shoot your goddamn knee into pieces so you'll never walk again!"

Spur let his hands go and stepped back.

"He's a fancy one, Pa. You said he was mine."

"Got to teach the bastard a lesson first. Take off his gunbelt, and be careful."

The girl slid up beside Spur while the old man covered him with his six-gun. She unbuckled the gun belt and pulled it off to one side, then she rubbed his crotch and his fly.

The old man swatted her to one side and slammed the side of the pistol into Spur's belly. This time Spur saw it coming and deflected it, swung once at the smaller man, but missed and took a sharp blow on the jaw with the side of the six-gun. He dropped to his knees, his head groggy.

The girl prowled around the area and came back.

"Just the one horse, Pa, but he's got two repeating rifles. A Spencer and a Henry! I get me the Henry, you promised me I could have a new gun."

"Yeah, yeah. Now you want this one, you hurry. We got to move on."

The girl moved up close to Spur where he sagged on all fours. She knelt in front of him and unbuttoned the last two fasteners of her shirt and let it swing open. Spur was eye to nipple with her breasts. They were the cleanest part of her.

"You like them?" she asked softly.

Spur blinked, trying to make the four breasts collect into two. At last they steadied. He nodded.

"You want them, first you got to play my game. You slap me. I like to get pushed around a little sometimes. Go ahead, slap me."

Spur slapped her gently. She slugged him in the side with her fist. It was a kidney punch and he almost gagged, but breathed deeply and sat back on his haunches.

"Slap me hard!"

He swung at her and his open handed slap spun her around and dumped her into the dirt.

She came up with tears in her eyes nodding. "Oh, yes! Do it again!"

"No."

A six-gun roared and the slug drove into the ground an inch from Spur's thigh and buried itself.

"Hit the crazy bitch!" the old man bellowed.

Tears in her eyes glistened as she nodded.

Spur hit her, jolting her into the dust again. There would be a bruise on her cheek. She got up quickly and crawled to him, rose to her knees and pushed her breasts into his face.

"Chew on me! Bite my tits. Make them hurt!"

Spur looked at the old man who had one hand filled with a .44, the other rubbing his crotch.

Spur did as she demanded, all the while trying to figure out this trio. The girl called him Pa, but that meant little. He doubted that she was this couple's child. She looked more like a new toy they bought or stole.

Spur realized he was chewing on good sized breasts yet he was not excited; he was as soft as a marshmallow.

"Yes, yes that feels good. Take my shirt off."

Spur left her breasts and took off her shirt. Her breasts were smaller than he had first thought, but still a handful. She pulled his leather vest off one arm and told him to drop it. Then she unbuttoned his shirt fasteners and snaked it off him.

She played with the black hair on his chest and smiled.

"We're going to have a party! Do you know that? A fine party, and we're going to get undressed and go over there in the grass where it's soft and we're going to just have a fine time!"

She rubbed his crotch, but found no erection.

"What's the matter, don't you like me?" She pulled open his belt, then unbuttoned his pants and reached inside.

The old woman snickered. "Got a big one but he must like little boys better than pussy, I bet!" She cackled and slapped her leg.

"Shut up, you old dried up crone!" the girl screamed. Then she smiled as she looked back at Spur.

"You just need a little help, some pussy help!" The young girl slipped out of her skirt that had been cut off around her calves, short for that time. She twirled it in front of her a minute and he saw that she had nothing else under it.

Her hips and belly were starkly white against the soft suntan brown of her back and chest. Even her breasts were tanned.

She knelt in front of him, took his hand and rubbed it between her spread legs.

"Now, you do like it, don't you, pretty man?"

Her blonde hair crotch was soft and damp and as she pushed his fingers against her outer lips, Spur could not help but feel his own hot blood surging.

"I don't believe this," Spur said softly.

"Believe, honeybear. You can have all of it you

want for as long as you want it!"

Her hand went inside his pants and came out with his long hard erection.

"Yes! That is more like it!" She stroked it once, then tugged at his boots. He had to help her with them. Then she stripped down his pants. When they both were naked the old woman hooted and shot twice near Spur just to see him jump.

"You crazy old loon!" the girl screeched. "You're just jealous you don't have tits anymore!"

The girl took Spur's hand and led him near the creek under some trees to long, soft grass and pushed him down. Then she lifted him.

"I want you to do it standing up!" she said. "Nobody has ever been able to fuck me standing up. Try it."

She spread her legs and Spur bent down and tried to enter her, but it didn't quite work. Then he bent over and grabbed her around the waist.

"Put your arms round my neck and hold on," he said. Spur lifted her off the ground. Her legs went around his waist and she used one hand to guide his turgid tool as he positioned her, then slid her forward, impaling her with his lance.

The girl laughed and screamed.

"You did it! You did it! First time ever standing up!"

The old woman shot twice into the tree. "Hurry it up, fucking young whore. Let a real woman get to him."

But the girl did not answer. The way they fit together put her clit under pressure with every stroke and soon she was reeling and wailing and jolting through a climax.

She went from one satisfaction to another and for five minutes she kept up the series of climaxes until she hung on him, spent and wasted.

Spur couldn't remember if he had shot his wad or not. She sagged off him and he let her slump to the ground. She panted, then went and sat in the creek where it was only a few inches deep. The cold water revived her.

The old man walked near her, his six-gun out. "What's the matter, you didn't call me. Weren't you ready yet on this one?"

She shook her head and smiled. "No, I want to keep him for a while, a few days at least."

Grunting with unhappiness, the old man went to Spur and tied his hands in front of him with wet rawhide. Spur knew at once that when the rawhide dried it would shrink up and cut off all circulation to his hands. He could lose his fingers in a big hurry!

He also knew there was no sense in trying to talk the rawhider out of it. He would as soon shoot Spur as tie his hands. Spur had to be patient and wait. There had to be a time to make a break for it.

Any of them would kill him for the horse, saddle and the two repeating rifles. They had nothing to lose.

The three rawhiders had a late breakfast then, and Spur could smell venison steaks frying over a small fire. They did not offer him any food or coffee. He knew better than to ask. When the food was gone, the old woman snarled at the girl to get things cleaned up.

The girl had put on her skirt but was still topless. She spat something back at the old woman who threw a tin plate at her. The girl held the fry pan with the venison drippings, and she swung it and threw it at the old woman. The hot grease splattered on her bare arm bringing a wail of fury and hatred.

"That was the worst mistake you ever made, slut!" the old woman screamed. She grabbed a foot long butcher knife from the cooking box and moved toward the girl.

"Don't start it!" the girl yelled. She reached behind her, found a six inch blade the old man had used for skinning the deer. It was sharp as a razor. She caught it in her right hand and waited for the older woman.

After two swipes with the knives failed to find flesh, the pair moved away from the fire and the wagon to a circle of grass.

"Put up with your mouth and your big tits long as I can stand!" the old woman bellowed. She slashed in with the knife, missed and stumbled away. The girl darted after her and before the old woman turned, the girl sliced her left arm near the shoulder bringing a crimson flow down the dirty shirt sleeve.

The old woman did not make a sound. She turned and glared at the girl, touched her wounded shoulder, then advanced.

The old man had seen the fight start. He moved over beside Spur, sat in the grass and chewed on a stem of grass.   •

"Seen it comin'. Bound to happen. Old woman just shriveled all up. Picked up the girl most a year ago now. She growed up nice. Taught her how to sex myself." He laughed. "That made the old woman mad as hell."

The women circled each other, each looking for an advantage. Spur sensed that the older one would die. The girl had all the advantages of mobility and strength. There was no way he could stop it.

The old woman charged the girl, darted in one way, then the other and continued the first way and sliced an inch long gash across the girl's left breast.

She screamed and jumped back. Holding the bleeding breast, her anger rising.

"Picked up the girl when her parents fell on hard times. Actual their whole farm and house fell on hard times, and hot times!" He laughed remembering. "Leastwise we took the girl and raised her a year. Built them girl bodies damn good back there. Now she's a real looker."

The girl moved with a purpose now. She went on the attack. Her first charge produced a new cut on her opponent's right arm, then one on her leg.

The girl kicked off her skirt to give her more mobility. She fought naked like a frenzy, slashing, darting in and out. She took one small cut on her leg, but paid it back with a six inch slice through the old woman's shirt and blood pulsed down her stomach staining her dress.

"Enough?" the girl demanded.

The old woman shook her head. She looked at the old man for a moment, then charged at the younger woman, trying for a fatal blow a thrust into the heart or lungs.

The strategy backfired. The girl accepted a small cut on her left arm as she caught the knife and powered it upward. Then her strong right arm drove the skinning knife deep into the old woman's chest. She pulled it out and stabbed her again.

Both stood still for a moment. Then blood seeped from the old woman's mouth, her eyes went wild searching for life.

The girl screamed a message of victory and slashed the razor-like skinning knife across the old woman's throat. She tried to gasp, but no sound came from her mouth. She fell, the knife dropping from her hand. She hit the ground and a rattling of her last breath gushed out.

The girl screamed again, dropped to her knees beside the dead woman and stabbed her chest a dozen times. When she finished and sat back, her hands and torso were bloody. Her breast still bled. She had blood on her legs.

She stood on wobbly legs and walked to the old man. There she lay down beside him, spread her legs and held out her arms to him. "Do me! Do me right now the way you taught me!''

The old man had been rubbing his crotch during the fight. Now he dropped his pants and drove into her. The girl climaxed again and again and when the old man came away from her she was so exhausted and drained that she slept at once.

He stood, picked up the rifles and two pistols, threw Spur's food sack and equipment sack on the horse and kicked Spur in the leg.

"Let's go," he said. Spur rose and looked at his clothes. The old man shrugged, cut Spur's tie and let him dress. Then he tied Spur's wrists again with dry rawhide.

The moment the horse moved, the girl sat up, then came to her feet and grabbed her skirt and ran to catch up with the other two.

None of them looked at the old woman where she lay in death. She no longer existed, her body was not their problem.

A quarter of a mile down the trail a small valley opened to the left and the wagon sat in it, concealed behind some brush. A small camp had been built with a cooking fire ring, forked sticks and two make-shift benches.

At the camp, Spur's horse was tied with the rest of the string on the lead line. Then the old man tied Spur's ankles together.

"Don't want you running off 'till we decide what to do with you. Thought we had decided that, but 'parently not." He winked at Spur. "Ain't she a cracker! Tits like I ain't seen in years and that snatch of hers just grabs you and won't let you go till you do her good and proper."

Spur only shrugged at his captor. He wasn't expected to reply.

Just after a cold noon meal, the girl came to where Spur lay under a tree. She offered him a biscuit with homemade jam on it, and fed it to him a bite at a time even though he could have held it in his tied hands.

"You was good this morning," she said, big open blue eyes measuring him. "Pa said I shouldn't feed you. No sense wasting good food, he said. But I been figuring me some. Pa is gonna have nigh on to four, five hundred dollars once he sells the string. I could get most of it." She looked up at him and shrugged.

"You know what I'm talking about, pretty man?"

"Not entirely."

"Trying to figure me out which one of you to go with. Pa—he's got the rig and horses, and I know him." She rubbed her hands over his bare chest and down to his crotch.

"But, Lordy, you got something a lot better to fill me up and make me scream in the night. Course you're younger, but, Lordy how you can love!" She watched him. "I never use naughty language. My folks were honest, hardworking people."

She sat closer to him. She wore only the skirt which now she hiked up around her waist.

"Feel my titties, pretty man," she said. She lifted his hands to her breasts. He rubbed them and petted them until she sighed.

"I could do lots better if you untied my hands. I could pet you both spots."

"Pa would whip me."

"He'd never see, you move over a little bit."

Her eyes widened, and she licked her lips. He tweaked her upright nipples and brought a gasp of pleasure from her. Slowly she took a small pen knife from her skirt pocket, opened it and without looking at the old man, sliced through the rawhide thong.

Spur rubbed his hands and wrists. She did the same for him, then when the feeling was back, he touched her breasts and with one hand touched her leg under the skirt and worked up.

The old man lay down in the shade and a few minutes later Spur heard him snoring.

The girl was beathing heavily then, scratching at his crotch.

"Do me!" she said. "Pa won't care. When he sleeps like that takes a thunderclap to wake him."

"Want me to tie you up and pretend I'm raping you?" Spur asked.

"Lordy! Yes! Ain't never had that done. Tie my hands first."

Spur did with the rawhide. Then he took off his shirt and tore off a strip off the tail.

"Have to gag you so you can't scream and yell," he said. She looked puzzled.

"If I'm raping you I don't want your folks to hear us, so I gag you so you won't scream and tell them."

He kissed her, then probed with his finger between her legs and she nodded.

He put the gag around her head and over her mouth so it wouldn't choke her. Then he bent and cut the thongs off his ankles. He tied them around her ankles, then kissed both her breasts and laid her on the grass.

Spur looked at the old man. He still snored. He touched the girl's cheek.

"Don't struggle too much. The old man will let you go when he wakes up." Spur stood, slid the Spencer out of the wagon and found his Colt .45 and gunbelt. Then he stuffed his shirt tail in his pants. He walked to the end of the trail line and untied his horse. A moment later he swung up and walked the mare out to the road and turned south. There were still three hours to sundown. With any luck at all he should be in Fort Smith before it got too dark to find his way.

He needed to touch base, and to get some new

supplies. Getting away from the rawhiders with his horse and guns was enough for one day. He wasn't going to push his luck!

CHAPTER SIX

NINE

When Spur rode into Fort Smith, it was nearing ten A.M. the following morning. In the darkness the night before he had lost his way in the thickets, missed a turnoff for Fort Smith and become hopelessly lost. He decided to spend the night along a small friendly stream deep in the brush. He had survived the night.

Now the Secret Agent rode into a dust filled conglomeration of dirt streets and one and two story wooden buildings, most of them unpainted, that went by the name of Fort Smith, Arkansas. He heard there were about 2,500 people in the town which had both a railroad and docks for river traffic along the Arkansas river.

More than twenty saloons catered to the trailmen and river rats, as well as a flood of cowboys halfway back home after driving cattle up the various trails to Kansas for shipment to the eastern markets. A good number of settlers also picked Fort Smith as a spot to jump off for points West.

Fort Smith began as a real army fort built on the site in 1817 and long since abandoned by the military. Now the fort buildings themselves remained a hollow shell, a large squat structure enclosed by sturdy stone walls with cannon emplacements on top. Adventurous children often played there, at night down and outers sometimes slept there and robbery victims often ended up breathing their last gulps of precious air before their deaths.

Spur realized he looked little better than the rawhiders from whom he had just escaped. He had not shaved in four days, he had not been able to take time to wash himself or clean his clothes.

Respectable women crossed the street when they saw him coming. A drunk swore at him, and Spur got no response from a man in a black suit when he asked where he could find the telegraph office.

At last he saw the railroad tracks and followed them to the station and the telegraph facility. Spur pushed into the small room and found no one there but the operator.

The man with wire rimmed glasses perched on his nose and a green eye shade, pushed back the garters that held his sleeves in place and glowered.

"Get your bones out of here before I call the sheriff!" the small man roared.

"I would appreciate that, sir," Spur said with his most polite tone of voice and his cultured, Eastern diction.

The telegrapher squinted and cocked his head.

"Would you say that again?" he asked.

"I would appreciate it if you would ask the sheriff to come here, since that is my second point of business today, to look up that lawman and hold a conference with him."

"Ummm. What's your first business?"

"I'd like to send a telegram." Spur lifted his Colt .45 from the holster by the barrel, pushed all five rounds from it and lay it on the counter top near the telegraph operator.

"I wish to send a telegram and have no funds. You may hold the weapon until I get money to reclaim it."

"We deal on a cash only basis."

"Sir, I am a federal lawman working in disguise. I wish to contact my office in Washington, D.C. for identification and an introduction to Judge Parker where I will draw funds. I hope we have no problem over this small matter."

The telegrapher looked Spur steady in the eye. Spur stared back at him openly with no threat.

"I think we can arrange that," the small man said. "Write out your message. 'Course as a goodwill gesture, I will retain your piece until you bring the money. No offense meant."

Spur smiled. "No offense taken. A prudent man is a good man." He wrote the message on a piece of paper with a stub of a pencil from the counter.

"Gen. Wilton D. Halleck, Capitol Investigations, One Pennsylvania Avenue, Washington, D.C.

I am without funds in Fort Smith, Arkansas. Please wire Judge Isaac Parker here my credentials and authorization to draw funds. Have contacted subject. Group number reduced to three. Urgent need here. Reply soonest. Signed C. Spur McCoy."

He handed the message to the telegrapher who read it, nodded and told him the cost. Spur motioned to the weapon. The man in his fifties grinned and turned to the key.

Spur heard the key stop chattering and go clear for a moment. The Fort Smith operator jumped on while he could and clicked out the message. Then he signed off. Spur had watched him, saw the man look up and nod.

"It's on the wire. Depends how fast the people in

Washington get it delivered. Sometimes they move quickly to government offices."

Spur thanked him and looked at the two wooden chairs. He avoided them and sat on the floor leaning against the wall.

"I'll wait. I have nothing else to do until that message comes in. Then I'll be glad to deliver it to the judge."

"Don't usually work that way," the telegrapher said.

"But you can do it this time, right?"

"Reckon so. Looks like you need a nap. Want some coffee? Got some warming in back."

"Please, then I might take that nap."

The telegrapher brought Spur a hot cup of coffee.

"You been in the Territories I'd guess."

"Yes, kidnapped, shot at, trapped in a circle of grass fire, tracked, trailed and within an inch of being blown straight into hell. When I go back in, things are going to be different."

The telegrapher nodded. "Sure as hell hope so. And I got to feel a mite sorry for the bunch you're looking for."

"The bunch has killed more than forty people already. Don't feel sorry for them."

Spur had sampled the coffee. It was twice as good as any he had made. He sipped it slowly, then leaned his head back.

The next thing Spur knew someone shook his shoulder. He came awake slowly, reached for his pistol but found only the empty holster.

"Mr. McCoy?"

"Huh? . . . Oh, yes. I'm awake."

"Your wire came through. I sealed it in an envelope for you and put the judge's name on the outside. Like I say, usually I take them over or hire a boy. Guess it will be all right this time."

Spur stood and stretched. Then he took the envelope, got directions to the judge's chambers and left the station. He found the courthouse, and the offices of the judge who had become well known in only four months of work here.

A deputy marshal stood in front of the judge's chambers. He drew his six-gun as Spur approached.

"Hold it right there!" the deputy marshal barked.

Spur stopped.

"What the hell you want in here?"

"I have a telegram for Judge Parker, then I hope to talk to him," Spur said with his best diction and his slightly affected Eastern accent.

The marshal blinked. "Sound a hell of a lot better than you look."

"Thank you. Will you see that the judge gets the telegram and tell him that Spur McCoy would like to see him?"

"Judge is busy."

"This is important."

The marshal laughed. "Everybody says that these days. I get dozens of people trying to see the judge."

Spur walked closer. "I'm a federal lawman. I've been working in disguise in the Territories. You've been in there, you know how rough it can be. This wire concerns me. It is of significant importance."

"Got any papers that prove you're a lawman?"

"Lost them back in the Territories."

"Possible." The marshal stared at Spur. "Damn if I won't give it a try. Can't promise. Sit down over there in that chair and don't move your ass a foot. I'll be back."

It was an hour before Spur McCoy walked into the private chambers of Federal Judge Isaac Charles Parker.

Judge Parker stood ramrod straight beside his desk. He was big for that day, six feet tall and two

115

hundred pounds. He was clean shaven except for a trimmed moustache and a neat but thick goatee. His straight black hair was parted on the right side and he stared with a hint of concern at McCoy.

"Judge Parker, I'm Spur McCoy. I hope the wire identified me and confirmed what I need."

"Mr. McCoy, I have my own deputy marshals who work in my jurisdiction."

"And I've heard they do a good job, Judge Parker. I'm on special assignment to end the rampage of the Jamison gang of bank robbers. They seem to be holed up in the Territories and I am authorized to go in and get them. I have no wish to usurp your command or your contol here."

"Secret Service," Judge Parker said softly. "Heard of it. Thought that was set up to handle counterfeiting."

"It was, sir. But then other problems came up and since we're the only real inter-state federal law agency, we have been overburdened with a hundred other types of crimes."

"Including bank robbers. Yes. I see by the St. Louis newspaper the Jamisons have killed forty-two people now in their rampage."

"Yes sir, but their gang is down from five to three. One was killed in Willow Creek, Missouri in a robbery, and I shot a second one in the Territories."

"You found their hideout?"

"No sir, but I know the general location."

"On the far side of the Territories?" the judge asked.

"No sir. I'd say it's not more than fifteen miles from your courtroom."

"That's outrageous!"

"I hope to do something about it, sir. But I need new supplies and a short rest."

"Yes. I concur. You look like you could also use a bath and some new clothes. Although your present ones would be a good costume for the Territories from what my deputies say.''

"Did you know there's a sign that posts a bounty on your deputy marshals? A hundred dollars I think it was.''

"The criminal mind is hard to decipher," Judge Parker said. "When I arrived four months ago I had ninety-one cases waiting on my calendar. I've hardly made a dent. I work twelve hours a day, but there is progress.''

He reached in his desk drawer and took out a stack of twenty dollar bills. He counted out ten of them and handed them to Spur.

"Your General Halleck has instructed me to advance you two hundred dollars, no questions asked. He said he would reimburse the cost to me by post. Is there anything else I can do for you?''

"You might suggest a hotel with a good dining room. I haven't been eating too well lately.''

The judge allowed himself a small smile.

"I can recommend the Arkansas River House. Fair beds, and an excellent cook." He nodded and his smile grew slightly. "I'd say you had a slightly Boston accent.''

"Yes, sir. I put in four years up there until I graduated from Harvard so I picked up some of the twang. I grew up in New York.''

They talked for a while longer, then the judge seemed to be thinking about something else. Spur thanked him, and went out the door with the two hundred dollars deep in his pocket.

Spur wasted the rest of the morning buying new clothes. He concentrated on rugged trail outfits, a checkered wool shirt, jacket, a dozen pair of good socks and a small carpetbag. He bought two boxes of new rounds for his pistol and rifle as well. Then he checked in at the hotel, ordered a tub of hot water and soaked for an hour. He had a relaxing early dinner and sat outside the hotel in his new denim pants, checkered cotton shirt and leather vest and a new low crowned brown hat pulled down over his eyes, as he surveyed the little town.

The Federal Court seemed to be a big part of the town's activity. Witnesses as well as lawbreakers were being brought back from Indian Territory. The forays were made by teams of deputy marshals, five or six to a group who traveled together for protection, and took with them a wagon that worked as a jail and chuck wagon for the trip.

When six or eight teams came back with an average of twenty lawbreakers each, and maybe twice that many witnesses, it taxed the small town's facilities. Witnesses flooded the place and some slept in the jail because they could not afford a hotel.

Spur watched the flow of people on the boardwalk and moving up and down the dusty streets.

Then he edged his hat lower and watched a couple walk past him. He had not even bothered to put on his six-gun after getting it back from the telegrapher. It lay in his room on the dresser.

Now he stared in frustration at the couple walking past. The man was the same one he had chased in the brush with Rorick. He was one of the Jamisons!

The bank robber carried two pistols low on his hips. He walked with a fancy lady who flaunted her new self importance as if she were loving it.

Spur was torn between following them and trying to get a gun. He saw several men moving past with pistols, but to ask to borrow another man's side-arm was simply not done in a town like this.

McCoy moved behind the couple trying to figure out what to do. If only he had worn his gun! He was almost never without it. Now he was paying the price. The couple kept moving past shops and headed toward the edge of the business district.

The girl waved at a painted woman who stood in the door of a saloon urging men to come in.

They went down a street and then into the residential section. Spur could only figure that the woman was from a dance hall saloon. She would be a working girl, and the Jamison would be buying her services. But why the flaunting?

He followed well back as the couple turned one more corner and went up the steps to a small white house and walked in without knocking.

Spur was flooded with questions. Did the girl live there? Was she a proper girl? Why did she know the whore at the saloon? Had the Jamison rented the house, or bought it? How could he attack a house not knowing who else might be inside?

Spur ran back to the Arkansas River House Hotel and took his pistol and the Spencer and went down the back steps to the alley. Again he trotted the six blocks to where he had seen the Jamison enter the house.

For a moment he thought of going to get the sheriff, or to call on a half dozen of the Judge Parker marshals, but he decided not to. This was his job, and he would do it.

It had been late in the afternoon when Spur first saw Jamison, now he checked the sun and saw that it was fading fast. It would soon be dark. He was not sure how good a look Jamison had of him in the Territories. At last he decided he could not go to the door and bluff his way inside. Too risky. He would wait until darkness and hope that Jamison came out.

Now, could he pick the man off with the rifle? Spur needed a positive identification first. While he was trying for a sure I.D. on the man, Jamison could be shooting Spur down. He snorted at the advantages the criminal always had. He knew it had to be that way to protect the innocent. This man could be a look-alike for Jamison, but Spur had a feeling he was not.

Darkness came as Spur crouched in an alley awaiting some movement from the house. Jamison was probably in bed with the floozy and would probably stay there the rest of the night.

Spur wondered if he should break down the front door and crash in on them. Or should he slip in the unlocked rear door and catch Jamison in bed with his guns hanging on the bedpost?

Spur discarded both ideas. He had to wait.

An hour after dark, he saw the front door open and someone come out. The figure walked his way and he saw it was the girl. He slid out of the shadows and stepped in front of her.

"Miss, I won't hurt you, I just have some questions to ask you, I'm a law officer. Will you cooperate with me?"

She stared at him, the fright fading. He saw that she was young, no more than nineteen or twenty.

Slowly her head bobbed. "Yes, I've done nothing wrong. Want do you want?"

"The house, is it yours, a friend's, or rented?"

"It is rented . . . I . . . we rented it this morning."

"Is it furnished?"

"Yes."

"Who is the man with you?"

"Phil Johnson."

"You know him from before today?"

"Of course! He comes to town now and then. I've been with him six or eight times. He's thoughtful and tender. A gentleman."

"What kind of work does he do?"

"He's a cattle buyer. Goes up to Kansas a lot."

"Where are you going now?"

"To get some more whiskey. We drank up what we had."

"Do you usually work in a saloon?"

"That's not a way to talk . . ." She sighed. "Yes, The Silver Horseshoe."

"Is there anyone else in the house?"

"No."

"Does Phil have a gun with him?"

"Yes, he says it can be dangerous on the trail. He has two pistols and a rifle."

Spur reached in his pocket, took out his wallet and handed the girl a ten dollar greenback.

"What's this?"

"I want you to forget about Phil . . . Johnson and go back to the saloon. Was he paying you more?"

"Fact is he was, twenty dollars."

"Had he paid you yet?"

"Of course, business before pleasure."

"So you must made thirty dollars for the night you didn't even have to work. Did you know Phil's last name isn't Johnson?"

"It is too."

"Afraid not. His real name is Phil Jamison, he's one of the Jamison bank robber gang."

"I don't believe you!"

"It's true."

"Impossible."

"What's your name?"

"Hettie."

"Well, Hettie, you wait and see if it's impossible. I'm going to have a talk with Phil. If he doesn't start shooting, you win and I go back to my hotel and you can climb back in bed with him. If he starts shooting you get back to the saloon. Fair enough?"

She bit her lip, then nodded. In the darkness he could see only her pale face and darting brown eyes. She was barely five feet tall.

"You're wrong, Mister. I know you're wrong."

"If I am you made an easy ten dollars."

Spur lifted his Colt and checked it, then slid a sixth round into the empty chamber and let the hammer down gently on the live bullet.

He left the girl and walked up to the door of the small white house. Spur paused, then moved to the side of the door and opened it silently. He stood at the side of the door and peered around it. Inside a lamp gave off a soft glow. He could see no one.

He pounded on the door, then turned the latch and shouted.

"Phil! Hettie's been hurt! She says come quick!"

He paused behind the door jamb and out of sight.

"What the hell?" someone shouted. He heard feet hit the floor and some quiet cursing. Then a half dressed man rushed into the short hallway. He had no weapon.

"Phil Jamison?" Spur asked as he pushed into the open door, his six-gun cocked and pointing at the man.

In an instant Phil figured out the trick, dove back the way he had come as Spur's Colt roared. Spur raced into the hallway and edged up to the door that led off to where Jamison had vanished.

There was no doubt about who the man was now. The room would be a bedroom where Jamison would have his clothes and his iron.

"Give it up, Jamison. I've got three deputy marshals outside that window. The only other way is through me. You couldn't do it in the Territories yesterday and you won't do it here. Remember how Rorick went down?"

There was a roar of anger and three shots clipped the edge of the door frame. Spur edged back.

The next thing he heard was a window breaking. Spur darted into the room but the robber was already out the window. The black night closed around him. Spur edged up in the lighted room to look out the broken glass.

A slug tore into the window molding an inch over his head. He ducked back. Spur heard someone running and vaulted through the broken window, but he could see nothing. He ran to the dirt street and turned toward the middle of town. Spur saw no one in the blackness, heard no running footfalls.

He went back to the house. The girl in the alley had left. In the living room he found a pair of saddle-bags. In one of them was a packet of five dollar bills. It still had a bank wrapper around it that had printed on it: "Willow Creek Fiduciary Bank $5's... $500."

Spur pushed the wad of bills and wrapper inside his shirt and walked out the door.

Solid evidence, the kind Judge Parker liked. Now he had enough to hang all three Jamisons that were left!

TEN

Phil Jamison had jumped through the low window in the small white house as soon as he recognized the gunman as the man who had killed Rorick in the Territories. He landed on his hands and knees, rolled to his back and leaped up.

Phil charged down the street into the darkness. He had taken time only to grab his gunbelt as he left the house.

Now he stopped half a block away, panting and strapped the leather around his waist and adjusted the big .44 in the holster.

"Come after me now, you bastard!" Phil whispered into the blackness. He saw a man come out of the house to the street, look both ways and then go back inside.

Phil figured he wouldn't stay long, and he was right. Five minutes later Phil watched the same figure come out of the house and stride the other way toward the business section of the little town.

Jamison had no idea what happened to the woman he had sent for more whiskey. Hell, Hettie might have been in on it with that sneaky bastard. It had to be the same guy who had gunned down Rorick in the Territories. How he had escaped the flames in that meadow Jamison would never figure out.

He slipped into the house by the unlocked back door, grabbed his hat and jacket then saw that the saddlebags had been searched. The bundle of five dollar bills was missing. Hell! So what, there was plenty more in his poke.

He went out the back door silently with all of his belongings and hurried to the livery stable. He had put his horse there when he got to town so it would have the best care. He took more pride in that roan than he did in his guns. Her dark red color was special, the best he had ever seen on a horse.

Phil paid the wrangler at the livery, saddled the roan and was on the road in five minutes. He crossed the Arkansas river on the ferry making sure the lawman who had gunned at him was not on board. As he mounted on the other side of the river, in Indian Territories, he began planning.

Phil had told the rest of the family what happened when they surprised the stranger near the hideout two days ago. Told them how the guy stuck to them, soon began hunting them! Now he was certain the man was a lawman. He must have recognized him in town and followed him to the house. Then when Hettie went out, he came to the door. The sneaky bastard!

Phil was so furious he almost made a wrong turn, and the longer he rode the madder he became. When he at last swung into the small ravine where they had built the little corral for the horses he was sputtering with rage.

Will Jamison gave his son a long shot of whiskey, sat him down at the table and tried to get him calmed down.

"When you think you can talk straight, boy, you go ahead and tell us what happened in town."

Phil gave them the story.

Will Jamison frowned and preened his drooping moustache.

"You sure it was the same varmint who shot down Rorick?"

"Can't be sure, Pa, nohow. But that's the only way I can figure it. How else would he know to call me by name?"

"Could have asked that girl you had there."

"Yeah, told her I was Phil Johnson. But that don't matter, I seen him up close two days ago. He saw me too. Important thing is what the fuck we gonna do about it! I want to get the bastard! I want to shoot him six times right in his damned face!"

Will held up his hand.

"You go charging off on half cock like that and you'll wind up buzzard food just like Rorick did. You want that, boy? Now calm down, Phil. Take it easy. Let's plan this out, way we always do. Got to be a way to even the score here. If it's the same man, we owe him for Rorick."

Dale finished cleaning his rifle and he assembled it slowly, lovingly. Then he lifted his brows.

"I say we go into town separately, find out where this joker is staying and we take him out. Three of us so that should be easy."

"He's gotta be one of Judge Parker's men," Phil said. "They the only ones who can come after us out here. Why the hell don't we ride in and dynamite the jail or Judge Parker's courthouse in there? Yeah! We could blow up the damn jail and let some of those folks go free and put a big stain on that new judge!"

"That's dumb, Phil. You ever used dynamite before? I sure ain't. Don't know nothing about it and I don't want to learn. We could just as well blow our hands off with that stuff. Any raid on the jail or Judge Parker is out. We try that, we might get it done, but if we did, Parker would have a hundred men out here searching every square foot of these Territories."

Dale nodded. "Think Pa is right, Phil. We should stick to what we know. Forget about that gunner. He's just another lawman we got to go around. Hail, we been doing that for two years."

"Catches in my craw! Makes me madder than hell. Besides, he ruined my night with Hettie. Been waiting six months to get her bare assed in bed with them big tits hanging out."

Dale laughed. "Knew we'd get to it sooner or later. Hell, she'll still be there in a week. Take off a month and pump her six times a day until you get so tired you can't walk!"

They all laughed this time.

"Phil got a point, though," Will said. "Why not make some kind of a hit-back at them for what this lawman did? Got me to thinking too. If he was a Judge Parker man he'd have six or eight men with him. They always work in groups, remember all them wagons and six men riders we seen out here rounding up wanteds?"

"If'n he ain't with Parker, who the hell is he?" Phil asked.

"Could be a U.S. marshal from Missouri or some other area where we been visiting," Dale said. "Don't matter." He turned to his father. "What do you mean hit-back at them?"

"Still figurin'. Tell you in the morning. Time we turn out the light and get some shut eye. Don't you two fret none, your Pa is working out something that will let them lawmen know the Jamisons are around, and warn them not to try to tangle with us."

"Pa, we is down to three men," Dale said. "Really need five for our kind of work. You thinkin' of taking on some hired help?"

"Thinkin', Dale, thinkin'."

A few minutes later they rolled onto their bunks and Phil blew out the last kerosene lamp.

Over a breakfast of venison steak and flapjacks, Will Jamison laid out the plan for his two sons.

"I figure we owe them for Rorick and for Gabe too. But I don't want us to charge into something we don't know nothing bout, like dynamite. 'Stead, we do what we do best. We rob a bank, not just any bank. We rob the Arkansas Riverman Bank, right there in Fort Smith! We take out the biggest bank in Arkansas with Judge Parker and his deputies just down the block! How does that sound?"

Dale had just stuffed half a pancake in his mouth and all he could do was grin and nod.

Phil jumped up and screeched in approval.

"Yeeeeeeeeeeeha! I love it! Yeah! Great idea, Pa! When we going in?"

Dale got his food swallowed and he joined in.

"Best idea we ever had, Pa! Make them lawmen hunker back and think about us 'fore they say we can't touch really big banks. How much you think their safe would hold?"

"Don't know, twenty, forty, maybe eighty thousand in greenbacks. Nice sackful!"

"When we go in?" Phil asked.

"Right after breakfast," Will said. "We do it right. Phil, you'll have to stay out of sight or wear a disguise, maybe shave off your beard."

"No! I'll keep out of sight."

"We work it the way we always do. I'll get a room at the Railroader Hotel, that little one right in the middle of town. We'll work our plan from there."

They hurried finishing the meal, cleaning up, and then got on their horses and moved out.

Four hours later Will Jamison signed the register at the Railroader Hotel as Will Jefferson and took room 109 at the far end of the hall on the first floor next to the back door. That way they had three exits, front door, back door and the ground floor window.

Will looked out the window that opened on the street. Up the street a block he could see the Arkansas Riverman Bank. It sat on the corner lot. Will pulled binoculars from his carpet bag and focused. He could see the side of the front door and had a good view of the back door. Yes!

He met the boys who came on horseback and told them where the room was. Then he faded into the Bit and Spur saloon for a cool beer. He had no idea where they got the ice.

When the Riverman bank closed at three P.M., Will Jamison sat in a chair across the street reading the local weekly newspaper. He was sitting with the chair leaning back against the Fort Smith Hardware. Three other men sat there snoozing, talking or watching the women walk by.

Will watched over the paper as someone locked the front door of the bank from the inside, then let out two customers. When they were gone the same man drew a blind down over the door indicating they were through doing business for the day.

By four-thirty two men and one woman had left by the front door. Will had walked into the bank briefly about three o'clock, saw that there was no guard, there were three tellers, and two desks with bank officers behind them. A woman secretary or bookkeeper sat on the other side. Six employees.

Will closed the newspaper and seemed to snooze in the late afternoon sunshine. One more man came from the bank, then it was quiet.

At five o'clock Will stood, put down the paper and walked back to the hotel.

Dale was already there. Two men had come out the back door, a young man and an older one who made a big production of locking two locks on the outside of the rear door.

"The older guy had to be the president," Dale said. "He wore a good suit that must have cost him thirty dollars! He even had one of them English hats on, a derby! Looked like a Fancy Dan to me."

"Chances are he opens the bank in the morning by the back door. Probably the same young man will be with him and he is armed. Won't matter none. Phil and I will be at the back door if he opens it there from the outside. Dale, you cover the front door in case he opens it there. If he does, you get him and the gunman inside without attracting any attention."

"He'll come in the back," Phil said. "Bet it's a habit with him. He parks a rig out there in the alley, so he'll come in and out the back door."

"Knew we had you in this room for something," Will said. He looked at him. "Told you I got you a surprise, you ready?"

Phil nodded. "Since I can't go out of the room it better be a good one."

Will went to the door and opened it. Hettie walked in, nodded to Will and Dale, then ran and kissed Phil.

Will and his oldest son went to the desk for another room, then for dinner and some serious drinking.

Spur McCoy had spent the previous night catching up on his sleep alone in a good bed, then that morning he went to see Judge Parker, made a report about the sighting of Phil Jamison in town, and turned in the five dollar bills with the bank wrapper from the robbed bank in Missouri.

The judge had it recorded and entered in the record, then went into his courtroom.

Spur watched the proceedings for a few minutes. The jury had just been selected in a murder case. The accused had killed the man he was traveling with for his gold watch.

Spur edged out of the courtroom. He still felt washed out and hungry. Maybe he was losing his enthusiasm for fighting the bad guys and the rain and heat and mud on the trail.

Naw!

He had a steak for dinner that noon at the hotel dining room and figured he'd have another one for supper. He decided he needed one more day of rest before he went back after the Jamisons. They would not be moving anywhere for a while. They also needed two more men to make their bank robbing team as efficient as it was before.

He stopped for a cold beer at a bar and asked them about the ice. The barkeep showed it to him, a block two feet square and four feet long. He kept it in a big wooden trough that had been wrapped with thick wool comforters. Dozens of bottles of beer stood around the cake of ice.

"Insulation," the barkeep said. "Keep it all wrapped up and a piece that size will last for three or four days."

"River ice?" Spur asked.

"Right. Let it freeze in the winter in our ice pond, cut it up with saws and haul it out and put it in the ice house between thick layers of straw, then cover it up with straw. We usually have good ice here until the end of September. Fact is we're running low right now."

Spur thanked him, drank his bottle of cold beer and lost six dollars in a small stakes poker game. Then he went to bed alone and slept ten hours.

Phil Jamison had been right. The president of the bank pulled his rig into the spot behind the big brick bank building, met a man next to the corner and quickly unlocked the back door.

They were not quick enough. Will timed it just right, running from the alley as Phil came from the other way. Will slugged the gunbearer on the forehead with his .44 and pushed both men inside the bank as the door swung inward.

Phil shoved the unconscious man to the floor, stripped his weapon away from him and quickly tied him hand and foot with rawhide stripes and put a gag in his mouth.

The president was a small man, in a three-piece expensive blue suit complete with gold chain across his vest and a gold watch in each vest pocket.

Will backed the man up against the wall, pulled the watches from his vest pockets and shoved them in his own. The ugly snout of his .44 pushed hard upward into the soft spot between the bones under his jaw.

"Open the vault, right now!" Will snarled.

"Can't, I only have half the combination."

Will slapped him hard, rocking his head to one side.

"My name is Jamison, Will Jamison. You may have heard of me. I specialize in bank vaults."

Sweat popped out on the man's forehead and cheeks. His florid face became redder.

"Yes . . . yes, I've heard of you."

"So open the safe before you have a fatal accident. Reckon even Judge Parker can only hang a man once." Will chuckled as he watched the man. "Open it!" The .44 jammed upward until the man lifted to his toes to decrease the pressure.

"Yes! . . . Yes, I can do it."

Phil ran to the front door, saw three people standing there waiting. He let them in. And showed his pistol.

"No problems! Do exactly what I tell you."

The two men held up their hands. The woman

shivered.

"Any of you have guns?"

They all shook their heads.

"Good, lay down on the floor and spread your hands as far as you can reach. Now!"

They did. He expertly tied all three, hands behind their backs, feet tied tightly. Then he put gags in their mouths. Someone knocked on the door.

Phil looked up and saw another bank employee waiting. He opened the door, tied and gagged him as he had the others. No sounds were made. Nothing would seem unusual from the outside.

He opened the bank door again, then closed it quickly. It was the signal. A moment later Dale walked across the street, entered the bank and locked the door again.

The boys hurried back to the vault.

It was one of the large ones, with two locks, but now it stood open.

"Please!" the banker said, standing at one side as Will dumped drawers full of U.S. greenbacks into a sack.

"A lot of good people are going to be hurt, ruined if you do this."

"Should have thought of that when they trusted a bank," Phil said. "Now shut up!"

"But if you take just what you need . . ." Phil drove his doubled up fist into the banker's soft gut and he bent over. Tears gushed from his eyes, he groaned in pain. When he stood up he held a Derringer he had taken from his pocket.

The first shot from the Derringer slammed into the sack of currency and the sound made all four men think they had gone deaf.

Phil drew first and sent two rounds into the banker's heart before he could fire again. They watched him slump to the floor of the vault and saw him die within seconds.

"Beat both you guys!" Phil said grinning.

They knew the shots would be muffled by the vault and the brick building. Still they hurried now. They emptied the vault of every dollar of paper currency, looked at two drawers full of gold coins.

Phil shrugged and took six of them and put them in his pants pocket.

"For good luck," he said.

Dale checked the employees. They were all tied securely. The bank wasn't due to open for two hours yet.

The three went to the back door, looked out. They waited while two rigs went by, then made sure the door would lock behind them and stepped out into the alley. Each man carried a large brown sack about half the size of a gunnysack. They walked down the alley where they had left their horses, mounted up and walked their mounts out of town west toward the ferry.

No one paid any attention to them. They were a hundred yards from the ferry when a man stood up and stared.

"Goddamn, it's Will Jamison! The bank robbers!" The man drew a pistol and fired. The Jamisons returned fire, forcing the man behind a building. Then they rode hard for the ferry which had just docked.

They pounded on board the small ferry, ordered the captain to cast off at once and unlimbered their rifles as two men ran toward them with pistols.

Dale put a round just over the first man's head and he ducked behind a water trough. The second man turned and ran the other way.

The Jamisons laughed knowing there would be no pursuit. Not for a while at least. The ferry boat captain guessed there had been a robbery. The man alternately scowled and smiled from under a battered yellow oiled cloth cap. He battled the current of the rain swollen Arkansas for several minutes, then coasted into the calmer waters near the far side.

"Boys, I don't take sides in these matters. I just carry folks back and forth. None of my business. See, I don't want trouble. I ain't armed. I just don't want no trouble."

Will had put his pistol away and leaned against the little pilot house.

"I don't make it a habit to give folks any trouble," Will said. "Usually make it a point to mind my own business." He grinned. "Course I do give them bankers a mite of unhappiness. But everybody knows them bankers got too much money for their own good." Will laughed and the captain of the little boat joined in.

When they were across there was no one waiting to come back. The captain tied up the ferry at the rickety dock. The Jamisons led their horses off the ferry, then Will gave his reins to Dale and ambled down to the dock.

"You aiming to go back across soon?" Will asked.

"Depends anybody comes," the riverman said, looking around the trail's end.

"Be a good idea if you don't go back over there," Will said. "Could be a posse that wants to come looking for us." He drew his .44 and shot the riverboat man in the forehead. He was dead as he splashed into the water.

An errant current lapped against the boat, and when the captain surfaced, the waters twirled his body around and sent it toward the fringes of the faster water racing downstream.

Will untied the ferry, shoved it away from the dock and watched it catch the current, then spin sideways and shoot downstream with the current.

"Any little advantage," he said softly. "Man's got to take any little advantage that he can."

ELEVEN

Spur McCoy had been talking with Sheriff Kennedy of Sebastian County when a man burst in the door.

"The Jamison Gang just shot up the town, robbed the bank and took off across the river on the ferry!"

Ten minutes later Spur and a posse of ten men stood at the river and stared across. A witness said he had heard a shot on the other side, then seen the ferry drifting downstream with nobody on board.

"Far as I can go," the sheriff said.

"Not as far as we can go!" A heavy set man said walking up to the river. He had two pistols and a rifle. He pointed at the sheriff. "We got 'em this time, Sheriff Kennedy. I'm Maxwell. I'm heading up a team of six Judge Parker marshals. We got our rig already on a boat ready to push off. We'll be on the other side in twenty minutes and not thirty minutes behind them!"

"I want to go with you," Spur said.

"We don't take strangers. Find your own damn boat." Maxwell snorted, turned and strode off.

The sheriff shrugged.

"Them marshals play it just about any way they

want to. Lots of small boats up by the dock. Somebody'll be glad to run you across for fifty cents. Looks like we lost our ferry boat and our boatman."

Spur thanked the sheriff and headed back to the hotel for his gear and to finish putting his traveling kit together. He would be more than thirty minutes behind, but he had a hunch Maxwell had not come up against Will Jamison before. He would be in for some surprises.

It took Spur a half hour to find a boat to take him and his horse across the surging waters of the Arkansas river. Rains upstream had raised the level of the water to near flood stage. When they docked at the ferry landing on the far side, Spur gave the man a paper dollar for his trouble and moved north expecting that would be the route the Jamisons and the marshals had taken.

To his surprise he found no tracks to the nine horses or the marshal's wagon. He turned and rode south on the north-south route and quickly picked up the prints. With the marshals' mounts and a spare or two, plus the wagon tracks, Spur could tell little about which tracks were whose.

He followed the trail south for two miles, then heard rifle fire ahead.

Ambush, he figured. He rode hard for a half mile, then eased up as the sounds of firing continued and seemed closer. Just over a small rise in the train he looked down a long rolling valley that angled toward the river.

A marshal's wagon was a quarter of a mile from him, stopped dead, with three of the marshals on the ground under and around the sturdy rig in what looked to be a defensive firing situation.

He spotted two dead horses then two more which were still in the harness for the wagon. Quickest way to stop a chase is to kill the wagon. Good thinking by the Jamisons.

The ambush had worked that far. One or two of the spare mounts might be used in harness. It depended how far ahead the marshals had planned.

Spur heard firing now from the left, nearer to the river. Some of the Judge Parker men must have pushed the attack against the ambush and driven them off and pursued. Good cavalry tactics if you had enough trained and mounted men. Three against three would not be good attack odds.

Spur pulled down from the two of the rise on the reverse slope and rode toward the river. He found some light woods he could use as cover and moved closer to the rifle fire. It began tapering off, and by the time he wormed his way to the edge of a patch of heavy woods, all the firing had stopped.

In front of him he saw two mounted men helping a third man up to ride double. A horse lay without moving nearby.

The Jamison clan had no qualms about killing horses. Most cowboys and most western men considered horses like second cousins and almost never shot an animal on purpose. Kill the man not the horse, the cowboy said. The Indians and the Jamisons evidently took a more realistic attitude. Kill the man's horse and he can't follow you. Kill his horse and he becomes easier to kill.

Spur rode out slightly in front of the two marshals' horses so they could see him. He sat and waited for them to ride to him. The Secret Service Agent recognized Marshal Maxwell as they came closer. He had been the loudmouth at the river.

"What you staring at, civilian?" Maxwell bellowed as they rode up. He was the one who lost his horse and was sitting behind the saddle.

"Marshal Maxwell, my name is Spur McCoy. I'm a United States Government Secret Service Agent. I've already checked with your boss, Judge Parker. He's received orders from my boss in Washington

D.C. General Halleck. I've been trailing the Jamison gang for two weeks. I could have helped you on your problem here if you'd let me. How many men did you lose?"

Maxwell looked confused. He swore softly. "Sir. We have one man dead, and one wounded. They ambushed us, killed our wagon horses, the bastards."

"You have any replacements?"

"One and a saddle horse. We can just about get the rig back to the ferry and then go for replacement animals."

"Sounds reasonable. When you get outfitted again, move north up this trail, not south. Their hideout is to the north about ten to fifteen miles, not too far from the border. I can always use some help with them."

Spur hesitated. "But if you come up there you'll be working under my control and my command. Check with Judge Parker if you want to. Otherwise, don't come."

"You some kind of a fast gun or something?"

"Something. I just don't like amateurs backing me. Maybe you should stick with the easy stuff out here. On second thought, tell Judge Parker that I'm requesting that he send no one to look for the Jamisons. If I'm not back at Fort Smith in three days, then he can send everyone he wants. I want your other two men to be sure that Judge Parker gets that message from me. Understood?"

The men nodded.

"Your names?"

"Flannery."

"Gerunding."

"Good. I'm moving back north. You men fell for the old broken wing trick by a mother bird when she leads you away from her nest. You better get your wounded man back to town."

Spur turned and rode north, moving along at a trot as he began to eat up the trail. He came on the tracks of three riders moving up the trail a mile past the turnoff to Fort Smith. They had circled around the wounded chuck wagon and jail rig and headed for home.

The Secret Service Agent checked the trail where the horses had crossed a grassy section. Some of the blades of grass were just starting to lift out of the crushed position. He was behind them only an hour, maybe forty-five minutes. He was too close to them. They would split up, or stop and set up another ambush.

He pulled off the trail, concealed his horse in a patch of thicket and sat down against a tree. Spur nodded and dozed and stretched in the sunshine for an hour, smoked a long thin black cheroot, and only then got back in the saddle.

A mile up the trail he found where the first of the horses angled off into the brush.

It was far too early for them to be going separately into their cabin. Spur guessed they were still ten to twelve miles from the hideout. He kept tracking the other two and when one of them angled to the same side and vanished into the brush, Spur pulled off as well.

He followed the trail in the soft underfooting. It was not the trail of a man trying to get away from trackers. Surely they knew someone would follow.

Trap!

They were laying an elaborate trap. Not an ambush this time. They must know the territory well and were heading to a spot where they would have a sure kill on one or ten men following them. Any one of the three trails would lead through the trap. They all were well ahead and would double back, be waiting to close the noose when the victims were inside the kill zone.

Spur rode slowly for half a mile, then hid his horse, took his Spencer and two extra tubes of rounds and moved ahead on foot following the tracks. He moved only a hundred yards when he saw the trail entering a depression.

He had been moving like an Indian, not making a sound, not letting a leaf crunch or a twig snap. He paused behind a shortleaf pine and studied the area below.

It looked like a natural amphitheatre. What looked like terraced, grass-covered wide steps led down to a central area that was flat and bare of all vegetation. On three sides the step-like risers worked down to the center. In back there was a great slab of granite that formed a kind of sounding wall.

Standing beside the wall and picketed on a short rope was one of the Jamison's horses. A brown sack lay on the ground as if it had been dropped. Spur lifted his binoculars and saw bundles of banknotes spilling out of the sack.

Tempting bait.

He began to look around the edge of the brush for the executioners. At least one had to be here, perhaps all three. He found one man to his left, almost at the same level he was around the rim of the bowl. The man's rifle glinted where the bluing had worn off, flashing a stab of sunlight Spur's way. Then it was gone.

Spur studied the position with his field glasses for five minutes and found him. A man lay in the brush and small green plants totally concealed him except for the light shade of his face. He stared Spur's way but not at him. He was watching where the trail came to the bowl.

One.

Spur looked the other way around the bowl. It

took him ten minutes to find the second man, and that was by chance. The man moved at just the time Spur studied the spot where he lay. Only his head and shoulders showed beyond a pair of ancient basalt boulders that lifted four feet out of the ground.

Two.

Spur could not find the third man. He could be close at hand. He might be half a mile away keeping the horses quiet. How long would the Jamisons man this trap?

Spur laid out several plans of attack. He could zero in on the easiest target with the Spencer. The range to each man was less than fifty yards. He could kill one of them for sure. But the other two would get away clean. Or when he gave away his position the other two might return fire and blow him into that long, long sleep.

He could put down the horse below. Cut down the mobility of the trio.

He could wait for them to make the first move, which would be to collect the horse and money below and move out. At that time he could kill the man below and the horse. Or he could wait and watch and follow them.

Before Spur had selected the best combat move, he heard a wild trumpeting sound and looked below just as a large, magnificent black stallion pranced into the clearing and watched the red mare next to the rock. She lifted her head and nickered. He moved forward. Behind him ten mares of various shades and hues came into the flat area. With them were half a dozen colts of different ages.

The rifle shot came a moment later. It chipped a shower of rocks off the face of the granite. The wild horses shied, then panicked and the stallion led them across the flat section, up the slope and into the cover of the trees and brush.

When they were gone, Spur looked back at the granite wall.

Both the horse and the sack of money were gone. One of the Jamisons had used the horses as cover for getting the bait and making a getaway.

Somehow they knew he was there, or sensed he was there. They were the ones trapped, and used this lucky romantic approach by the stallion to escape with no one injured and no losses.

Next time, Spur told himself. When he checked the sniper positions on both sides, he saw that they were empty. The shooters had pulled back and were well on their way by now. Spur lay where he was. They could still be ready to ambush him if he moved too quickly.

He looked up at the blue sky with just a few high feathery clouds. It was a good day for tracking, and there was a lot of it left. He would wait a half hour before he moved a step. Such a wait could very well be the difference between living and dying.

When he figured the time was up, Spur rolled over and stared around him. He saw nothing. He sprinted to the first large tree away from the natural amphitheater.

Nothing happened.

He rushed to the next cover, then the next until he had moved a quarter of a mile back toward his horse.

All clear. He jogged on to where his horse waited.

Now all he had to do was track them again. The woods or the trail? They would move quicker now, that would mean the trail. He guessed they would ride hard to the trail and for five more miles north, then lay a confusing set of tracks that only a master tracker or a lucky man could follow.

Spur would let them do that. He already knew

where their hideout was, at least within a mile or so of it. He would go around their tracks, back to his known position and move toward that small mountain meadow where he had first surprised Phil Jamison and Rorick.

Spur expected no trouble on the trail for the ten or twelve miles north. The Jamisons probably figured they had stopped any pursuit, had blunted the attack of Judge Parker's deputies, so now they would vanish into the hills and relax until their next bank job.

A record of their attacks showed that they had followed a pattern during the last year. They would be quiet for a while, then surge into the border states around the Territories hitting one bank after another, usually three to five, before things got so hot for them they staged a "forced march" back to the Territories where they disappeared. The time period between raids was from three to six weeks.

Spur rode carefully, but making good time. He trotted his mare for a quarter of a mile at a time, then walked her, then trotted her. In this fashion he covered the ten miles in a little over two hours.

A pistol shot behind him made Spur spin around in the saddle as he drew his iron. Twenty feet away a horseman had come into the trail.

"Don't shoot, old pardner. You didn't show up at our meeting spot so I figured I better come looking for you."

Spur relaxed and holstered his weapon.

"Longjohn Ferrier, the bounty hunter deluxe. I thought I lost you for good."

"Not with sixteen thousand dollars on the hoof out here and us closing in on them."

Spur told him about Rorick and how he nearly got killed by the rawhider women, and the robbery at Fort Smith.

"You get all the luck. So where are the Jamisons?"

"About two or three miles from here."

"Let's get riding."

Spur held up his hand. "Ferrier, you ride with me, I'm the general and you're the damn private. You do what I say or I'll be shooting you, not the Jamisons. Do you understand? I am going to capture or kill the Jamisons. I don't give a damn about your reward money."

Ferrier spun his revolver and holstered it. "Hell, all I want to do it pick up the pieces and take them in for the reward. That's after we level their hideout and wing them a couple of times. You general, me private."

"Remember that when the shooting starts. You move or stay or shit when I tell you to. Got that?"

"Yes sir, general sir!" Ferrier gave what he must have thought was a salute.

Spur grinned in spite of himself. "I just hope to hell that you're going to be more help then hinderance."

They rode down the trail. Spur had no trouble finding the spot where he had followed the tracks entering the woods two or three days ago. A half hour later he had let his "nose" lead him until he found the meadow.

"Right over there is where I surprised Jamison and Rorick," Spur said. "All we have to do is back-track them, but we do it slow and careful. Damn careful."

From there they both moved slowly forward.

Before he left Fort Smith, Spur had visited the hardware store and put together six sticks of dynamite. He fitted each stick with a thirty second burn fuse and a detonator cap. Then he bought big headed roofing nails and some sticky tape, and taped nails around each of the ten-inch long dynamite sticks.

When one went off it would be like a cannon filled with grape shot as those roofing nails exploded outward with the force of forty rifle shots.

They rode around the small meadow and found the double set of prints on the far side. It had been several days but hoofprints in the soft mulch under the hickory, oak and gum were still plain to see.

Spur and Ferrier worked ahead slowly, on foot, leading their mounts. Whenever there was a rise they tied the nags, worked up it silently and studied the landscape ahead. The third time they did this Spur saw a narrow gulley open to the left and what seemed to be a pole fence that had been built across it.

Spur worked closer until he was sure. Someone had made a corral out of the little gully. There were three horses in it, and all were still cooling out.

"Paydirt!" Ferrier whispered. "Their hideout's got to be close around here."

Spur and Ferrier left their horses tied to some brush. Spur stuffed four of the dynamite bombs inside his shirt and buttoned it again, then took his Spencer and three of the extra ammo tubes and moved to the far side of the corral looking for a path. He found several tracks, but no real path. The Jamisons must use different approaches each time.

He picked a trail and they followed it.

Spur and Ferrier moved like Indians again, never taking the next step until they were sure it would not make any noise. They checked a hundred and eighty degrees ahead as they walked.

A rabbit scampered away to the left. A blue jay and an owl ruffled their feathers to the right. Four times they stopped to listen, but heard nothing.

The next time Spur listened he heard a harmonica

giving out a baleful tune.

Spur grinned and Ferrier nodded. He patted his Winchester 1873 army rifle.

Hideout time!

They moved even more cautiously now.

The Secret Service Agent bellied down on a rise fifty feet from a small brook. Just across the stream lay a little clearing. There was no cabin, no building. But the area had a sense of being lived in. Then he saw a rack next to a tree. It was hung with strips of meat. Someone was making jerky!

Indians?

They would not hide their dwelling.

Spur looked more closely at the area. He took out his binoculars and studied it a section at a time.

Then an oblong section of the landscape moved inward, revealing nothing but a black hole.

A doorway?

Spur pointed at the spot then looked at the rectangle with the binoculars. Dimly he could see a door frame, then a glint of rusted hinges. He concentrated on the area until he could make out the shadowy form of a small cabin that had been built thirty or forty years ago flush against a tall, sheer rock wall. Trees and brush grew all around it.

Additional work had been done with cut brush to make it even more hidden.

A laugh drifted from the doorway.

"Fifty-seven thousand dollars!" a voice said clearly. "Almost twenty thousand dollars each!"

The voices faded then as someone closed the door.

Ferrier nodded. Both men realized they had found the hideout, and that the gang was inside. Now all they had to do was take them.

Spur stared at the objective. He motioned Ferrier back a little and they whispered.

"See that chimney on the far side? It must be for a fireplace. We'll blast them out. I'll drop the dynamite down the chimney. You be out here and knock them down without killing them. When they come wheezing and coughing out the front door. Remember, Judge Parker wants them alive."

"Easier to handle dead," Longjohn said. He shrugged. "Alive it is."

"If one of them breaks past you for the horss, you light out and follow him. Run him to ground and take him into Fort Smith. No sense trying to find me. Now pick your firing spot to cover that front door. You saw it?"

Ferrier nodded. Spur moved closer. They would have no guards outside. Why should they, they had been safe for two years.

He had spotted two windows, one on this end, one on the front. Both were small two pane affairs and high up. He could walk right up to the place.

Instead he moved up with cover as long as he could, then he crept to the side and came around the stone cliff to the side of the cabin.

He had spotted a stone chimney toward the back. It would be for a fireplace, and a straight drop into the hideout. He had a surprise they would get a bang out of.

Spur checked the sun. Five or six hours to sundown. Plenty of time.

The cabin had been built of chinked logs, sturdy hardwood logs that could last for a hundred years. The builders had not trimmed the ends leaving a convenient set of steps upward. Spur moved slowly, Indian quiet, making no noise at all on the log ends or the sod covered roof that sprouted brush and even a few small trees.

He worked forward slowly, laid down his rifle and two of the loaded ammo tubes at the edge of the roof over the door. Then Spur took one of the sticks of dynamite from his shirt and walked silently on the grass surface to the chimney.

The top of it was five feet above the roof. He found his packet of matches in his pocket, tore off one and lit the fuse. He let it burn for five seconds, then dropped the dynamite bomb down the chimney.

Twenty seconds later the blast shot soot and smoke out of the chimney. He heard the windows break and somebody scream as the rumble of the explosion died out in the heavy woods.

TWELVE

For a moment after the bomb went off inside the Jamison's cabin, nothing happened.

As the noise echoed through the woods, Spur heard a long chilling scream from inside the hideaway. The sound came out of the chimney, through both windows that had been blown out and through the door.

Spur was still moving toward his rifle when the scream took form and a man jolted out the door. His shirt was singed, his hair half frizzed and burned, and a long red tear on his cheek showed dripping blood.

He had six-guns in both hands and a saddle bag over his shoulder. The man was firing his revolvers as he charged out taking Spur by surprise. He sent round after round at the circle of brush around the cabin as he darted toward the nearest cover ten yards away.

Spur drew his six-gun and fired twice, but by then the man was in the woods. There had been no shots from the big bounty hunter.

"Ferrier, you asshole! Why didn't you shoot him?

He was yours! Now get moving and go chase him down. Wherever he goes you go until you bring him back! You hear me?''

Ferrier stepped from behind a tree thirty yards away and nodded. Then he drew his six-gun and charged into the woods after the fleeing man.

Spur was ready for the next one or two. He waited on the roof. Thirty seconds ticked past and no one came out. Had they both been killed in the blast? Not likely from one stick of dynamite.

Still . . .

Spur scanned the small clearing again, saw nothing. He could hear no movement from inside the cabin, but realized the foot of soil on the roof provided perfect soundproofing. He couldn't hear anyone if they were shouting.

He had to get to the ground and look inside.

Spur went down the log ends the way he went up. Window glass littered the dirt outside the small building. He carried the rifle in his left hand, and his six-gun in his right as he edged up to the door. It had been blown off its hinges and blocked half the entrance. Spur tried to look inside. He realized he was outlining himself in the outside light.

He looked both ways, then darted into the cabin. Smoke lingered in the air. A heavy layer of soot spread over everything. His eyes grew accustomed to the dimness quickly. Table, chairs, one tipped over. Bunks against the wall. An old kitchen cook stove with a stove pipe going into the fireplace stone chimney.

He squinted and checked it all again. No bodies. He had heard more than one man in the cabin. Probably three. Where were they?

Escape tunnel?

He looked for rugs on the floor. It was packed earth. At the far side under a bunk he saw boards that had been nailed together. They had been slid back in place but not far enough. Spur pulled them out.

A tunnel!

He dropped into it and crawled forward. For a second or two it was totally black, then six feet farther on he saw daylight. The short tunnel slanted upward at once and soon he came into the open behind a large patch of heavy brush.

Spur went to his knees and examined the ground. Bootprints, two sets. Two men had left. He also saw several drops of bright red blood that had not had a chance to dry yet.

Injured, wounded at least superficially. They both could still move. There was no foot dragging.

He moved ahead tracking them. Always tracking.

They ran at first. He could tell by the length of the stride, the way the heels and toes both dug into the leafmold. But gradually they had slowed, now they walked, moving steadily to the south. Why south?

Spur guessed they would run to the interior of the Territories.

Without warning the tracks turned east. Arkansas? Why would they turn that way?

Spur kept reading the sign. They were moving, making good time, there seemed to be no major injuries. He wondered what kind of weapons they had. Had they taken time to bring their money with them? He wasn't even sure if they had divided the last haul. The weapons worried him more than the money. Two Henry repeaters could throw out twenty-six rounds of .44 sized lead in one hell of a rush.

He came to a slight rise and scanned the country ahead. They were heading higher into the Brushy Mountains. Spur realized they had been climbing gradually for the last pair of miles. A small valley opened up below and a quarter of a mile down there he could see two figures moving slowly across the open area.

Five hundred yards. He could risk firing a half dozen rounds at them, but he was not sure how the Spencer was sighted in. He probably would only warn them he was trailing them. No. He would move in and nail one. Then they couldn't split up on him. He had to put down one, then go after the second Jamison.

Spur held the rifle at port arms and charged down the hill, running hard, making up ground on his quarry. He stayed under cover. They would be checking their back trail when possible. He was sure he could get within range before they made it to the woods on the other side.

He had seen a river coming down the valley, but he had no idea how big it was. Most of the creeks were small and easy to wade across. Anything else would change the Jamisons' plans in a rush.

He ran harder, then stopped to check the two fugitives. He had made up a hundred yards. He saw one turn and look back. Spur melted against a tree and remained motionless. The best way to be seen in the woods or in the open is to be moving. A still figure can be mistaken for a tree or stump.

Then he was moving again.

A hundred yards farther along he became aware of a sound. It was new. He listened again, and then he grinned. The small little stream ahead was not small and was not just a stream. What he heard was the sound of white water.

The river was going to pin the Jamisons on this side for some time. He would have a chance to catch them right here!

He ran hard again, then paused and looked down at the river. Here it was fifty feet wide and a boiling, churning melee of rapids and whirlpools and swiftly flowing currents. The rain earlier in the higher hills was now making its way toward the Arkansas river down this nameless stream.

Spur knew he had a chance to end it right here.

He leaned back on a rock and looked below. The two men were not in sight.

A rifle bullet chipped splinters off the rock he rested on and sang away into the brush. Spur rolled, grabbing his wrist where shards of the rock had gouged out a thumbnail of raw lacerated flesh.

He came up behind the rock and peered around it.

Now they knew for sure that he was after them.

Spur crawled ten feet to the edge of a patch of woods and lifted up behind an oak tree. He checked the spot the rock was struck and where he had seen the Jamisons before. They were slightly upstream from him.

Good. He moved in short rushes, as if he were in the Civil War again, running from one cover to the next, taking every advantage of the terrain he could find. He wanted to get closer to the river, about thirty yards away, then move upstream after the pair.

They had at least one rifle, so they probably each took weapons before they left. How much of the money did they bring with them? It would only be natural to take as much as they could.

Spur got to the point he wanted to near the river. The white water and the power of the current made him think trying to cross the water would be a last choice. He scanned the area ahead and saw one of the men dart from a huge rock near the water into a thick patch of woods.

They might be moving upstream where they knew there was a spot they could cross on the rocks. Spur stayed to cover and run to within thirty yards of the woods that he had seen the man enter.

He crawled up to the edge of the cover and watched. At first he saw nothing, then he saw someone building a blind with small pieces of pine boughs. Pushing them into the dirt, then leaning them against each other.

Spur sighted in on the figure and fired.

The figure screamed and rolled out of sight. Spur put four more rifle shots into the area, but heard nothing else. He finished the last shot and rolled a dozen feet to the left. Just as he left another rifle from up the line of woods riddled his firing position with four shots. Spur returned fire at the second gunman, then moved again.

He reloaded, pushing a filling tube of rounds through the base plate of the Spencer. Then he ran. He slanted downstream sightly to a line of brush that would put him into the edge of the copse of trees where the Jamisons hid.

He let them know he was coming.

They had no shot at him and would not give away their new positions.

Spur dropped behind a big oak tree and looked around it. He took one of the dynamite sticks from his shirt, lit it and threw it near where he had seen the first shooter. The bomb with shrapnel-like roofing nails taped to it went off with a sullen roar.

Spur could hear the nails zinging through the trees. There was silence after the blast.

Then Spur heard a laugh.

"Somebody really wants the Jamisons bad, don't they?" The voice came calmly, in a full and powerful tone. It was a mature man's voice.

"Will Jamison I'd guess," Spur shouted back.

"Close enough. How much is it going to take to buy you off?"

"More than you have, Jamison. I don't do business with killers who slaughter people for the fun of it."

"Then you'll die. We have you in a crossfire right now."

"Not a chance. It must be Dale I just shot. He's

hurting bad. Tell him not to try the river. Too dangerous."

"Christ, you think it's safer on this side?" The new voice was softer, younger. It must be Dale.

"You'll both get a fair trial in Fort Smith," Spur said. "You come in now and it might go easier on you. A trial later is better than being dead in half an hour."

"Don't see no help you brought to do the job," Dale said.

Spur had pinpointed the voices now. They were closer to the rushing sound of the water. He eased forward a dozen yards toward the voices to a tall pine tree and stood behind it.

"Have all the help I need," Spur said. "Mr. Colt and Mr. Spencer here help out a lot."

Spur moved as soon as he said it, swinging toward the water. Soon he could see the white rushing flood.

He could hear the men talking, but he couldn't make out the words. Then one voice lifted.

"Damnit, try it then!"

Spur watched upstream as near the voices as he could see. There was a stretch of fairly calm water that showed a strong current. As he looked, he saw a form splash into the water. Saddle bags were tied around the man's chest and he had a pistol in one hand.

It was the younger man, Dale. He went under water, then came up pawing water, his gun gone as the current rifled him toward the white water ten yards below. It was a series of two foot drops as the water roared and raced around boulders, logs and broken end snags that had been ripped free somewhere upstream and floated down.

Dale went under again, hit the white water and bobbed a dozen times.

Spur watched him out of sight where the river

made a sudden turn into green timber. He looked up stream. For just a moment he saw Will Jamison on a rock, then he jumped back out of sight.

The Secret Service Agent put a Spencer round into the rock, then moved silently forward. He came out on a pile of boulders near the shore and commanding a hundred feet of the riverbank.

Always take the high ground!

Spur checked the area. There was no sign of the older Jamison.

"Give it up, Jamison. You've got no place to run, nowhere to hide. You'll get a fair trial."

"And then I'll hang!" The voice boomed out almost below Spur. The rocks shielded him from the outlaw who stood near the water below the ancient boulders.

"You got a name? Man likes to know the name of the man he's doing business with."

"Spur McCoy."

"Well, McCoy. I've got a business proposition for you. I've got my saddlebags that are stuffed full of packets of hundred dollar bills. Hundred of them in a stack. That's ten thousand dollars to the bundle. Then I have a batch of packets of fifties and twenties.

"I'd say I have nearly eighty thousand dollars in those bags. How much do you make a year, maybe four hundred dollars, five hundred at the most?"

"About that."

"Half of all I got is yours. Say forty thousand dollars. That's almost a hundred years wages for you. All you have to do it catch the half of the saddle bag and turn and walk back to your horse. No questions, no contact, no problems. You get rich, and I reduce the work load on Judge Parker's hangman. What do you say?"

"Always wanted to be a rich man. How do I know

you won't shoot me in the back as I walk away?"

"My guns will be on the rock."

As they talked Spur worked forward on the boulder. He could not see Jamison. He began to work his way around the side. Then he slipped and rolled down the sharp face to the ground ten feet below. He lost the rifle but held on to his Colt.

As he flew through the air he saw Jamison leaning against the big rock. He was holding his left arm which was bloody. By the time he got his hand to his six-gun, Spur had hit the ground and rolled out of sight next to the base of the rock Will stood on.

"Your time is running out, Jamison," Spur said. He was edging his Colt up and over the rock when he heard the man laugh. He had moved.

"Years yet, McCoy. I'm an expert swimmer. Sure as hell hope you are." The splash that followed brought Spur to his feet and leaping up on the rock.

Will Jamison had jumped into the river. Spur saw the saddle bags tied around his waist. Jamison stroked on top of the water, then came to the small rapids and he went out of sight for a minute.

Spur had to chase him. He searched the shoreline quickly, saw what he wanted and ran for it. It was a chunk of pine log about six feet long. Spur rammed his six-gun in his belt, picked up the log and dragged it to the water. It was dry and light, would float well, and Spur hoped keep him alive down the river.

He slammed into the water with both arms around the log and his legs around it too with his ankles locked.

The shock of the cold water stunned Spur but he held on. Then he was on a wild ride downstream. The first twenty feet went fine, then the rapids jolted and banged him against rocks until he thought he would loose his float entirely. His legs came loose and he struggled to hold on.

Twice he went under water but the log popped back to the surface quickly. He gulped in lungsful of glorious air just when he needed it most.

In a quiet stretch he looked ahead but could not see Jamison. White water sounded again ahead, but this time he steered himself around the worst of it going down one more abrupt drop but into a good pool at the bottom of the three foot fall.

Another quiet spot, but he saw no one.

Ahead he saw a blue shirt. He looked again. Dale Jamison was holding onto a snag that stuck out of the water. As he came closer, Spur realized Dale was not holding on to it. His head was under water and his body wedged in a "V" created by two logs that were wedged in rocks.

Two Jamisons to go.

The white water grabbed him again, jerked the log out of his grasp and drove him deep into a pool that had a whirlpool effect. Spur had to dig in with his crawl stroke and kick with every ounce of effort and strength he had left to get out of the whirling water.

Then he floated on the surface resting, not able to kick toward shore.

Again the white water tore at him, slammed him against one big boulder after another, and soon he learned to try to catch the rocks with his hands to buffer the blow.

He was almost out of them again when his head banged on a rock and he thought he was going to pass out. He fought it, splashed and clawed at the water to keep his head above the surface, then once more the water slowed and calmed as the river bed flattened out.

To his left was a narrow sandy beach. He kicked and tried to stroke that way. The current tugged at him, refusing to let him go without a battle, but when with one flurry of desperation kicks and fast strokes with his arms, Spur surged out of the current and drifted slowly up to the sandy shore.

Spur dragged himself up until he was half out of the water and lay on his stomach panting. His face rested on his arm on the warm sand, and for just a moment he knew that he had been near to drowning. He panted and sucked in all the air he could.

It was ten minutes before he felt strong enough to sit up. Twenty feet down the small beach he saw gray pants and a gray shirt.

Will Jamison!

Spur struggled to his knees, felt for his Colt in his belt. It was gone. He might still have the Derringer deep in his back pocket, but he was too tired to reach for it. He pushed himself to his feet and took slow steps down the sand.

With every movement his toes dug in the sand leaving long trails. The body had not moved since Spur spotted it.

He made the tremendously long walk, then fell to his knees beside the body. He had to identify it.

When he rolled Will over, his eyes came open and he coughed, spitting up water and wheezing.

He lay on his back, his eyes closed sucking in air.

"If this is hell, it don't look too bad!" Jamison said at last. He was too weak to lift his hand.

Spur sat beside him, legs out straight, his trail shirt still waterlogged and ripped by the force of the current. He took it off and wrung it out, then put it back on but could not manage the buttons.

"You almost made it," Spur said.

Jamison nodded.

"You saw Dale."

Tears seeped from the father's eyes, his head nodded once.

A half hour later, Will sat up.

"I'm taking you back to Fort Smith," Spur said.

Jamison laughed. "How you plan on doing that? Neither one of us can hardly walk."

"I'll manage." Spur stood. "Let's go, it's a long walk."

"Can't get up."

"Like hell you can't. Try."

Jamison moved his hands, tried to stand, dropped down. Then he turned and in his hand he held a derringer. Spur had reached with his left hand to help Jamison just as he fired. The .45 slug that should have hit Spur in the heart slammed through his left arm, broke the bone and glanced to the side into the water.

Spur automatically kicked out with his water logged boot, hitting Jamison's right wrist, slamming the derringer out of his hand and sailing it into the river.

"You broke my damned wrist!" Jamison shouted.

"Good, you broke my arm. Now get on your feet and let's walk."

"Hell no. You gonna kick me all the way to the gallows?"

Spur lifted his own Derringer which he had fished out of his pocket and shot Jamison in his left shoulder. Jamison roared with anger and pain holding his wounded wrist, then his shoulder.

"You bastard!"

"True, let's go. I have one more shot and I'll put it right through your right eye if you try anything. Dead or alive the posters say. I don't collect rewards anyway. You'll be out of circulation either way, that's my job. Take your choice."

Will Jamison stood slowly, glared at Spur and moved away from the river.

"We'll go back to the north-south trail and look for a ride from somebody. Hate to see you all worn out when we get back to Fort Smith and we have a parade in your honor down main street to Judge Parker's jail."

THIRTEEN

Spur stopped the march after half an hour. Will Jamison had three wounds in his left arm and wrist. He carried the arm tucked in his shirt. Spur did what he could with one hand to stop the flow of blood from Jamison's shoulder and arm.

Then he bound up his own left wrist. It still burned like fire. He had lost enough blood so he noticed it, and now the broken bone began to move. He had cut off one sleeve of his shirt and used it as a bandage and wrapper around the bloody hole where the bullet had ripped in and through his arm.

There was no chance to make a splint that would work. He closed his eyes for a moment to let the continuing pain filter away. The broken bones scraped against each other and every step brought a new jolt of pain.

Jamison was as tough as Spur figured he would be. Spur kept him walking ahead. They found the north-south trail after another half hour and took another break and rested. The battering fight and struggle down the river had drained more strength from them than they first suspected.

Spur hoped that a farm wagon would come along, but none did. Deeper into the Indian Territories were more than fifteen thousand whites, all living there illegally. Some of them just moved in and began farming and ranching. Others had married Indian women and taken over what land they wanted.

A few claim that they bought the land from friendly Indians who had no real right to sell it. Little was done to move the whites out of this Indian preserve. There were tougher, more demanding problems.

But as chance would have it, there was no farmer wagon going to Fort Smith this evening.

The sun worked closer to the horizon. Spur kept the Derringer deep in his front pocket. It was his one control over Jamison. Without it they would have a bare knuckle fight and probably neither of them could win it in their condition.

Spur heard a horseman coming, but when the rider saw the pair on foot he slanted through the woods and went round them. Just before dark a pair of riders came by.

Spur held the Derringer now aimed skyward.

"Evening. We shore could use some help. Would you ride us double down to the Fort Smith ferry?"

Both the mounted men were fresh into the Territories, they were too clean to be long time residents.

"Why the hell should we do that?" one of them asked.

"Get out of here," Jamison shouted. "He's a goddamn bounty hunter."

The men laughed and whipped their horses down the path.

"You just cost yourself a ten mile walk," Spur said. "I dont' know if you're going to make it or not."

"So what? Longer I can put off Fort Smith, I

figure is the longer I get to live. Also, I'm counting on Phil to come back and blow your head off so we can ride north."

"He the one ran out of the cabin?"

"Scorched the poor guy across the face. Damned vicious thing you did back there, McCoy, that dynamite."

"I fight fire with fire. I never do anything to an outlaw that he hasn't done, or wouldn't do if he thought of it."

Jamison snorted but kept walking.

"Never have trusted black powder. Now I sure as hell don't like this new fangled dynamite."

The sun had just rimmed the far landfall when a horse came up the trail heading north.

Spur moved Jamison into the brush and watched. The man on board moved slowly, and trailed a horse with a rider who had his hands tied to the saddle horn.

When the rider came nearer, Spur stepped into the trail.

"About time you're getting back, Ferrier. What took you so damn long?"

Ferrier grinned. Phil Jamison rode the horse behind him.

"You like a lift?" Ferrier asked.

"We both would," Spur said.

Will Jamison came out of the woods.

Ten minutes later Ferrier had rebandaged both men's wounds. He helped Spur into the saddle on Phil's horse and moved the outlaw behind Spur. Then Will lifted into the saddle behind Ferrier and they moved south. Ten minutes later it was dark.

They fired two shots from the dark ferry landing opposite Fort Smith and a light blinked at them, then they heard a boat coming across.

The boat chugged up to the dock a short time later and they all walked on board. Ferrier shouldered a pair of saddlebags he had taken from Phil Jamison. He also gave Spur his six-gun to help hold the prisoners.

"Suppose I got to turn in this saddle bag," Jamison said.

"Yeah, I suppose so," Spur said.

"I could have lost it out there, then went back and found it when all this robbery talk quieted down."

"True. I never did find Will's saddle bags, or Dale's. They must be in the river or on the shore or maybe in the Arkansas river by now."

Ferrier grinned. "Now that would be finders keepers if I stumbled on it one of these days."

"Technically the cash should be turned in."

"Ain't never been very technical. Besides, it's a damn treasure hunt. I love a good hunt." He took the saddle bags off his shoulder and draped them over Spur's right shoulder.

"I'm giving you almost twenty thousand dollars," Ferrier said. "Just a few seconds ago I was a rich man."

"You have eight thousand on the hoof right here," Spur said. "When I get patched up a bit we'll go back and get Rorick and Dale. That should be another eight thousand. You'll still be rich and you won't have to look over your shoulder the rest of your life."

"Yeah, right. You just struck yourself a bargain."

"Them guys the Jamison bank robbers?" the new ferryboat man asked.

Spur said they were.

"Damn! Gonna be a celebration tonight! You got back the money, didn't you?"

"Some of it."

"Yeeeeeeeha!"

As soon as the boat tied up, the ferryboat man ran into town spreading the word that two Jamisons had been caught. A half dozen sheriff deputies and a hundred men and women poured out of the saloons and gambling halls to watch the little march to the court house and the jail.

Judge Parker arrived to welcome his two famous guests. When it was all over Spur told the Judge that Ferrier deserved the rewards on the two.

"You give me about a day to get patched up and I'll lead a team of your deputies back to the cabin. Must be some of the money hidden around there somewhere. Rest of it is in the river."

"The other two in the gang?"

"Both dead, Judge. I shot one three or four days ago, and the other Jamison, Phil, drowned in the river yesterday."

"We'll need both bodies for the reward."

"Yes sir, we'll bring them in." Spur swung the saddle bags to the judge. "Here's about twenty thousand of somebody's money. The bank wrappers might still be on it. It's all yours."

"Fine, that's a start. Now, you better get yourself to a doctor." Judge Parker paused. He preened his goatee with his right hand and nodded. "Yes, McCoy, that was good work. I'll send your General Halleck a wire commending you."

"Will you need me as a witness in the trial, Your Honor?"

"Yes, it would help." He paused. "I'll schedule the trial for early next week, four days from now. That way you won't be held up here too long."

"Thank you, Your Honor."

The doctor waited for Spur in his front room offices at his house just off the main street.

The medical man was an old hand in the Fort Smith area. He unwrapped the shirt sleeve and looked at the mangled bones and the blue welts just under the skin.

He took a bottle of whiskey off the shelf and poured a glassful for Spur.

"Is it that bad, Doc?" Spur asked.

"Yes. Back in Boston I had all the sul-ether I wanted to use, but there just isn't any supply of it this far west. It will be used routinely someday. Did you know that ether was used on a towel during an operation in 1841? Here it is almost thirty-five years later and still a country doctor can't get it." He indicated to Spur he should drink up. When the glass was empty the doctor filled it again.

Two hours later Spur was so drunk he could hardly keep his eyes open. He hardly noticed when the doctor pulled the bones apart, forced them back into position and treated the gunshot wound. The medic wrapped the arm tightly against a stiff pine slat on both sides of the gunshot wound, but left the injured flesh available for treatment. Then he cast the arm around the wound with plaster-of-paris.

The next morning Spur woke up in the doctor's spare bedroom, which constituted the only "hospital" in Fort Smith.

The doctor fed him breakfast, laughed at his hangover and then told him that Judge Parker wanted to see him. He declined any pay, saying he would charge it to Judge Parker's deputy account as he always did. The cost was a dollar for setting the bone, fifty cents for the whiskey, and fifty cents for the overnight stay.

Spur walked with unsteady steps for a block before he got his head straightened out. Then he moved quickly to Judge Parker's office. His lower arm felt like an anchor with all of the plaster on it. He had to get used to it since the doctor told him he had to leave it in the cast for five weeks.

Judge Parker had changed his mind.

"I want you to lead a search party for the rest of the money in the hideout today," he said. "You can ride in the wagon or on horseback up to the site. But we should move quickly on this."

"I'll send eight deputies with you. Ferrier will go, too. Since these rewards are federal I'll authorize payment from here, but we won't have that kind of cash to give him."

Spur agreed, had a huge breakfast at the hotel with Ferrier, and left with the eight Parker deputies at ten o'clock.

Spur rode his horse and carried a flask of whiskey to help deaden the pain.

The trip went smoothly. They found Phil's cache of money in his metal box under the first bunk, and took the box back to the wagon. The hideout revealed three more hiding places for money, and Spur did not bother to count it. Much of it was still in original bank wrappers, and would be returned in due course to the right bank.

At the river they had less luck. The deputies fished Dale from the water. He had the saddlebags still tied around him, but one of them was empty and the other one held only six bundles of fifty dollar bills.

They did not find any trace of Will's saddle bags or his money.

A deputy was detailed to follow the small river and check every sandbag and bend in the water searching for packets of bills or the saddlebags. When they met him later in the day, he reported he found only two twenty dollars bills.

Spur and two deputies followed the trail Spur had ridden in his chase with Rorick and Phil Jamison. They found the body almost where it had fallen. Carion birds had eaten at the back of his neck and one hand was gone. They threw the body over a trail horse, tied the hands and feet together under the mount's belly and headed for the ferry.

* * *

Two days later Spur was nearly recovered. They had come back with eighty-two thousand dollars from the hideout, and Judge Parker was pleased.

Longjohn Ferrier had drawn two hundred dollars, and had Judge Parker send his letters of credit for the rest of the sixteen thousand dollars to a bank in St. Louis where he would pick it up or deposit it.

Then Longhorn bought new camping gear and went back to the river where Spur assured him there was something like eighty to a hundred thousand dollars in U.S. banknotes. He was treasure hunting. He wasn't going to pass up a chance to really be rich!

In a way, Spur wished he was going with him.

That noon in the dining room of his hotel, Spur had a window table when a woman walked up and cleared her throat.

"A real gentleman would help a lady sit down," she said.

Spur looked up and smiled at the pretty woman. She had long, curly blonde hair billowing around her shoulders, wide set eyes and a pleasing smile. Something about the smile caught his interest. He stood at once and helped her sit at his table. He had not ordered yet.

She sat down, waited for him to sit and then smiled at him. "I bet you don't recognize me, Mr. McCoy."

Spur slid into the chair, mesmerized by the beautiful woman across from him. She wore an expensive dress, her hair was combed and brushed until it shone like gold threads and her pretty face had just a touch of color added, but not enough to brand her as a painted dance hall girl.

She was dressed as a grownup woman, but Spur had a feeling she was younger than she seemed. Seldom had he been so attracted to a female. When her soft blue eyes looked at him, Spur wanted to start spouting Byron's love poems. That was ridiculous, he told himself, then he looked up at her beautiful face again.

"Mr. McCoy. I said I really didn't think that you know who I am or where we met."

"Uh . . . no, I'm afraid not. Usually I never forget a beautiful woman. Will you have dinner with me? I was about to order."

She smiled. "Yes, I will have dinner, thank you."

Spur signalled and a waitress brought a menu. She looked at it a moment, then ordered a steak dinner with three side dishes.

He watched her, but nothing hinted to him where he had met her or when. He had seen few of the town's women, certainly none to say hello to or be formally introduced. Absolutely not this beauty.

"How did you hurt your arm? Is it broken?"

"Yes, I'm afraid I was shot, but it's nothing serious." He sipped at his coffee. "Are you going to be in town long?"

"It depends. And you?"

"For most of the week. Legal matters."

Their food came and he was amazed at the way she made the thick steak disappear. He stared at her without apology. The dress she wore covered her to her chin and wrist, but it hinted at such loveliness underneath that it was more provocative and sexy than a gown that showed half of each breast.

At last he put down his napkin and reached for her hand.

"I'm sorry! I don't even know your name. Now that is unfair, you know who I am. What do I call you?"

She laughed and the sound touched his memory but nothing came clear.

"My name is Irma, Irma Woodhouse. Does that help your memory at all?"

Spur did not mind the teasing. He would have begged her to tease him so he could stay near her.

When the meal was over she stirred as if she were getting ready to leave.

"Please stay a moment," Spur said. "I'll go out of my mind if you don't tell me where we met. Was it here in Fort Smith?"

She shook her head and stood. Spur hastily paid the check and offered her his arm. They went to the lobby where she sat down in one of the upholstered arm chairs and indicated he should sit beside her.

"Before I tell you where we met, you must promise me something."

"Of course, just name it."

"I'm going to be in town for the next week, and I want someone to show me around, to take me to any plays or concerts that might be on, to go with me when I buy new things at the shops, to be my escort and guide. Could you do that?"

"For a month, a year!" Spur grinned. "Well, for as long as I can. I do have to be at one of Judge Parker's trials, but when I'm not there . . ."

"Good. Now, if you'll walk me up to my room, I'll tell you where we met. I just hope you don't change your mind."

Her room was on the second floor. She unlocked it and stood watching him.

"My real name is Irma Woodhouse, but I haven't used it for almost two years. I met you about a week ago in Indian Territories." She watched him closely. "My ma and my pa got killed and I lived with some other folks . . ." She reached out and touched his hand. "I was with the rawhiders, the old man and old woman who captured you . . ."

Spur's head snapped up in shock, surprise and wonder.

"You . . . the same person with those rawhiders?" He shook his head, walked away three steps, then came back. "It's totally unreal. How could you change so much? How did you get away from them . . . from him?"

She opened the door and walked into her room. He went after her but left the door open a foot. She sat on the bed and watched him.

"Yes, I'm the same Irma. My real ma and pa were killed by the old man, and they took me. I was only fourteen. We was going to Oregon but got lost from a train up in Kansas a ways. The old man shot my real pa, then raped my mother and killed her." Irma brushed her hand over her face.

"They took me and made me work, and the old man kept bothering me, and then one night he undressed me and started 'training' me about sex. At first the old woman screamed at him but gradually she didn't mind. I was just a kid then. But now I'm all grown up."

She wiped tears from her face. "I just sort of went along with them, it was easier. Then you came and it changed things. I told you I was trying to figure out which one of you to go with. But you tricked me and ran off."

"Next thing I tied up the old man while he slept. I took all the money he saved in his hiding spot, and I took ten of the horses and got all cleaned up, washed my hair and combed it and all, and came to Fort Smith. I sold the horses and got a room and took a bath every day and had my hair fixed, and then I bought some new clothes.

"Tonight I saw you sitting here, and that's it. Spur McCoy, I want you to help me learn how to be a lady!"

Spur kissed her cheek and then paced the room. He thought about the old woman and how she died. He thought about the wild, erotic way Irma Woodhouse had made love to him. He thought about the kidnapping of a girl and her introduction into crime and sudden death and rawhiding at its worst.

"Yes, Irma, I'll be happy to help you become a lady. The fact is, you're a lady right now. I don't know what I could do for you that would make you any more of a lady."

"Lots, you can help me lots. What my real Ma used to call the social graces. I ain't gone none. Teach me how to walk, and to talk to people, and what to say and how to act with strangers." She took a deep breath. "Teach me that I can't just jump in bed with every nice looking man I see." She was gritting her teeth. "Like I want to do right now with you!"

Spur stood and took her hand. "A lady does not allow strange men in her bedroom. So I'll step outside." He did. "Tomorrow morning my cast and I will call for you and we'll go shopping. I need some new clothes, and you can buy something. It will be a start."

Tears streamed down her cheeks. "Thank you," she said. "Maybe now . . . . maybe now I can turn out to be decent the way my mamma would have wanted me to be. At least now I have a chance."

She held out her hand to say good night. Spur shook it gently, then bent and kissed her lips with a feather touch and moved back quickly.

"While you're refining the techniques of being a lady, I'm going to have to use all my will power to try to be a gentleman. That's so I don't charge into your room right now and tear off your clothes!"

Irma smiled, then laughed softly. She closed the door and Spur heard the key turn in the lock.

He turned and walked down the hall toward his room on the third floor. It was going to be a frustrating afternoon and evening. Irma Woodhouse was the same female who had ravaged him in the Indian Territories! He was still in a state of shock.

He had business to keep himself occupied. First he

went to the telegraph office and wired General Halleck the results of his campaign and that Judge Parker requested him to stay and testify.

Then he went to the closest saloon and stared at one beer after another trying to make sense out of it. Irma Woodhouse was the same woman, the same sexy, erotic female he had mated with in the wilderness. He wasn't sure that he would be able to keep his hands off her for the next four or five days. He was not sure that he even wanted to try!

FOURTEEN

The next morning Spur slept in. His arm hurt. He had a headache. He did not want to play gentleman to a nymphet cum lady in the training stages.

He shaved and dressed, had breakfast at the ridiculously late hour of eight, then bought a new white shirt, a string tie and dark blue jacket. At least he could dress like a gentleman, even when he wanted to crawl between the sheets with the lady.

Christ what a lady!

Spur had himself under control by ten that morning when he called at Irma's door in the hotel. His arm cast would not fit into the coat sleeve so he had the casted arm in a sling and left the left sleeve hanging empty. It gave him that wounded soldier look.

Irma opened the door and he sucked in a quick breath.

His brows hadn't come down yet when she laughed. She was stunning. She had piled her long curly blond hair on top of her head showing off her slender neck and highlighting her coloring. The dress she wore was a simple print frock, but it made

Spur want to see exactly what it was hiding.

"Astounding!" he said at last. "I can't believe that you are the same woman I knew so well in the Territories."

"I could remind you about that mole you have three inches below your belly button." Irma grinned and he laughed.

"It's you, all right. I should get rewarded with at least a small peck on the cheek."

She caught his hand, pulled him into her room and closed the door. Then Irma put her arms around hs neck and pulled his head down and kissed his lips with fire enough to launch a cavalry attack. Her breast pressed hard against his chest and one knee lifted and gently rubbed his crotch.

When she let go and stepped back she giggled. "There, that's your reward for today. It's going to have to make do for the whole day, though."

Spur touched at a bead of sweat on his forehead.

"That will more than do. If you want to stay safely inside that dress, I'd advise you to get out of this room and stay in public until I get cooled off!"

She opened the door and went out, waited for him, then took his arm after he had closed and locked her door.

"First we are going to that little dress and hat shop just down the street. I bought this dress there, but I need something for the theatre tonight. I asked. There is a company of Shakespeare players in town and they are performing tonight at eight P.M."

Spur fumbled for something to say. "I tried out for *Hamlet* once in college. Those old Englishmen talked too fast for me. I couldn't even understand what they were saying, let alone memorize all of those lines."

"Who is *Hamlet?*"

He told her. "This will be your Shakespeare

education, so remember all of it. That will put you a dozen steps ahead of ninety-five percent of the other ladies in this town."

Spur sat in the outer sales room at the milinery and dress shop while Irma tried on three dresses. She bought all three. One cost four dollars, the second five and the third a silk dress that seemed to be the best in the shop, was fourteen dollars. The lady was making some alterations in it and Irma could pick it up later that afternoon in plenty of time for the theatre.

Outside Spur stopped Irma in front of a lawyer's office.

"Just how much cash did the old man have that you relieved him of?"

"I don't think I should tell you."

"Why?"

"You'd get mad at me."

"A lady would say that I would become angry with you. But I won't. Just curious. You're spending it like you have thousands. Do you know you just spent more than a month's pay for a working man?"

Tears edged into her eyes, and he turned around and screamed silently at himself for being such a clod. He looked back and the tears were gone.

"Sorry, none of my business. That old rawhider stole two years of your childhood. Nothing is too much to replace that."

"Almost six hundred dollars," she said softly.

"Six . . ." Spur laughed. "I'd like to have seen his face when he got untied and found his treasure missing."

"I did. I told him before I left. He almost had a seizure. Until you came along, I thought everything he did was right. I guess he had me hypnotized or something. I was under his spell."

Spur smiled and touched her hand. "Now I'm

under your spell. Where are we going next?"

"I thought an early lunch. I hear some ladies call it lunch instead of dinner when we eat at noon. You know, breakfast, lunch and dinner. The Eastern way of saying it."

"Yes, I've heard of that. The hotel or somewhere else?"

"The ladies said there is a nice little tea room down the block a ways that is run by an Englishman who came over here only a few months ago. He has a delightful accent."

They had tea and biscuits at the little shop. It had a British air about it. Two Union Jacks, pictures of London, a portrait of Queen Victoria held honored places at each end of the room.

The man who ran the tea room did have a delightful English accent. Spur talked to him a moment and soon discovered that his real name was Porloski and he was from Massachusetts. He had been a merchant seaman for a time and spent a year in England between ships. The tea shop sounded like a good idea.

Spur never did tell Irma.

A messenger tracked down Spur in the general store where Irma was buying a new set of combs and a hand mirror.

Spur read the note and caught Irma's hand.

"Judge Parker wants me in his courtroom right away. It will be a special hearing to charge the Jamisons. I'm one of the witnesses. This will broaden your knowledge of the court and justice system in the nation."

The hearing was underway when they arrived, but they were taken into the room and seated. The judge was informed Spur McCoy was there.

Two of the bank employees who had witnessed the robbery and seen the accused had testified. A third took the stand but broke down when asked to recall if he could the shooting death of the bank president. He testified that he had not actually seen the shots fired but said he had heard the younger Jamison say that he had beaten both his father and his brother in shooting the bank president.

The witness was excused and Spur called to the dock.

He was sworn in, then the judge stared at him for a moment.

"The court recognized Spur McCoy as a special law officer sworn to the United States Government. Did you capture these two accused?"

"I captured one. The second was apprehended by Longjohn Ferrier. We delivered them to your jailers."

"These men both had stolen bank notes on them when you captured them?"

"They did, Your Honor."

"The witness is excused. This court finds just cause to bind over the accused for trial. Said trial to commence Monday morning in this courtroom at 8:30 A.M."

Spur smiled as he led Irma out of the courtroom.

"That's what I like, quick movement of the law. In New York it would have taken three months for that case to come to trial. There would have been lawyers all over the place. This is a lot cleaner, faster and more satisfying."

"What if the judge makes a mistake in all the rush?" Irma asked.

"Then the wrong man is imprisoned or hung. But that doesn't happen often. I'll go along with Judge Parker, quick justice for murderers and rawhiders, and let the outlaws beware!"

"That was some speech."

"I might run for Congress. Now what are we going to do next?"

That evening after they came from the town hall

where the company of four put on several bits and pieces of Shakespeare, Spur was footsore and weary. His arm had been aching all afternoon and he wanted a shot of whiskey to help kill the pain. Now a new pain arose but he pushed it down.

She was so lovely his groin ached.

Irma held out her cheek. "You may kiss me goodnight, if you don't think it's too improper."

He pecked her cheek, then reached round and pecked her on the lips but withdrew quickly.

"I think I better get out of here or your standing as a lady in town will be seriously jeopardized." Spur nodded to her and closed the door quickly. He noticed that she did not lock it behind him. He reached for the knob, but stopped just in time and turned and walked down the hall to his room.

Saturday and Sunday, Spur squired the prettiest lady in town to every social function, half the stores in town, and to church on Sunday. He never more than held her hand all that time, and he was starting to wonder if his arm or his crotch was hurting more.

Sunday night he stood just inside the door of her room, his foot wedged in the opening to stop the door.

She stood close to him. He noticed she had worn some perfume tonight and it had clouded his mind all evening.

Irma touched his cheeks and tenderly kissed his nose.

"Spur, I don't understand. You know what I want to do. I guess for the last two years I just thought everybody had sex whenever they wanted to. Now it's different." She put her arms around his neck and moved close to him so her breasts pressed against his shirt.

"Don't nice ladies ever make love? I mean they must if they have babies, right? I know what causes babies. So nice ladies must do it . . . sometime."

"With their husbands. Nice girls don't make love until after they are married. That's the key word. Get married and you can jump your husband twice a day and three times at night. It's perfectly respectable then."

"Oh, damn!" She scowled, then in a moment she brightened. "But what if nobody knew!"

"No. You said you want to settle down here in town, find yourself a husband and raise a family. Good. Then I'm not going to endanger any of that with a jump into your bed. It's just not worth it. So forget it."

He pulled her arms away from him, pushed her back a foot or so and edged out of the room. Before he closed the door her face came up close.

"How about a quick little kiss goodnight?" she asked.

She pushed her face into the opening. He leaned in and kissed her lips gently, then pulled away and closed the door. Again she did not lock it behind him.

The trial opened Monday morning on schedule. The charges were bank robbery, murder of the bank manager, and the murder of the ferryman in Indian Territories.

Spur sat with Irma watching the proceedings. The Judge said he would call Spur the first day so he could be on his way.

Judge Parker had a special situation in the Federal Court of the Western District of Arkansas. The former judge had been such an incompetent that he failed to cover up his own bribery and was forced to resign in the spring of 1875 or face impeachment and a possible prison term himself. Over ninety cases had stacked up that had not been tried by the former judge. Congress was thinking of combining the Western district with another one.

Then suddenly Congress had an ideal replacement in Judge Parker. He knew the situation and actually *wanted* the job! President U.S. Grant appointed him to the vacant judgeship and Congress quickly approved. He had arrived in Fort Smith on a riverboat on May 2, 1875.

By late September he had his legal machine functioning efficiently. The first eight weeks all cases pending had been tried and six men had been hung for murder. The springing of the trap in Fort Smith was music to the law abiding citizens' ears.

The judge's courtroom was so efficient mainly because there was no recourse to one of his verdicts. The normal channels of appeal were not open because most of the cases originated in the Indian Territories, which in effect was an independent nation, and outside the Constitutional guarantees. Only a direct pardon by the President of the United States could negate one of Judge Parker's sentences.

They were all jury trials. The jurors drawn from the working folks of the Western Arkansas area who were sick to death of the lawlessness in the Territories and in the western Arkansas counties as well. They went along with the judge's quick justice ideas.

Many times when the judge did not like testimony, or when he considered it prejudiced or that the witness was simply lying, he would refuse to allow it to be heard. Judge Parker ran roughshod over slick lawyers who tried to get clients off, bulldozed others into not practicing in his court, and soon showed the legal profession that he was boss in his court and he would have his way.

A flyer detailing the laws governing the U.S. Marshal and his deputies for the Western District of Arkansas, was different from others in the nation.

In part it said: "U.S. Deputy Marshals for the

Western District of Arkansas may make arrests for murder, manslaughter, assault with intent to kill or maim, attempt to murder, arson, robbery, rape, burglary, larceny, incest, adultery, or willfully and maliciously placing obstructions on a railroad track.

"These arrests may be made with or without warrants first issued and in the hands of the Deputy or the Chief Marshal. It is always better for the Deputy to have a warrant before making an arrest, yet if he knows of any one of the above crimes having been committed and has good reason to believe a particular party guilty of the crime, his duty is to make the arrest."

Spur had heard that the deputy marshals drew two dollars for each arrest when the man was delivered to Fort Smith. The deputy got nothing for a corpse, unless there was a wanted poster on him with a reward. So the deputies shot to capture their suspects, not to kill them.

Spur settled down to watch the trial. As usual it got underway promptly at 8:30 A.M. and would be in session until nightfall. Now and then night sessions would be held. Judge Parker had plenty of customers for his justice.

No lawyer represented the Jamisons. Judge Parker appointed one who hardly knew his right hand from his left. The list of witnesses hastily drawn included bank employees, citizens who had seen the Jamisons leave the bank by the back door or on their ride to the river.

Again Spur testified about the capture of the two men, about the attack on their hideout, the subsequent drowning of Dale and the capture of the other two.

Spur was excused.

The outcome of the trial was a predictable one. Little evidence was given to show that the Jamisons had not robbed the bank or killed the president.

Spur and Irma left the courtroom and two new spectators eagerly rushed forward for their seats.

Late in the afternoon word came to the English Tea Room where Spur and Irma were eating. The Jamisons had been found guilty and would be hung the next day. Spur lifted his brows in surprise at the speed of the justice. It was fast even for Judge Parker. Then he heard that the two additional hangings would fill out a set of five that the judge would hang the next day.

Spur lifted his tea cup and sipped, then put it down.

"We were talking about Irma Woodhouse. She is a nearly grown woman. But she should have more education. You can read and write, and do sums, but these days a woman needs more than that. There are many women going into business, learning trades, becoming self sufficient. No longer is a woman tied to and must be dependent on her husband."

"But maybe I want to be dependent."

"Fine, but give yourself a choice. If you get married tomorrow and have five babies in the next five years, you will no longer have a choice."

"I have a choice right now. I could always be a fancy lady in a saloon. I know exactly what they do and how they do it and I'm trained to please a man and I must admit that I do enjoy making love."

"So you could have three options. Don't sell yourself short. You are a beautiful woman with a delightful young body. There are a lot of things you could do, if you want to try. But you'll have to make an effort."

"I've never seen a hanging. Can we go tomorrow?"

"Yes, a part of your education. It's not exactly a picnic but there will be wagon loads of people coming to town from all over the area. Sorry to say it will take on a carnival atmosphere. The trap drops at 9:30 A.M. Let's go down there now to the fort compound to look at the gallows. We won't be able to get anywhere near them tomorrow."

The gallows stood in the courtyard. They had been built especially to Parker's specifications. The posts and crossbeams were twelve inch square oak timbers. A narrow trap door ran the length of the platform. As many as twelve men could be hung at once with a single thrust of the lever dropping the trap door. Spur pointed all of this out to Irma.

Irma looked up at it and shivered.

"Judge Parker kills men here," she said. "Somehow it doesn't seem much different than what the old man did in the Territories. I mean, the men involved are just as dead no matter who killed them or how it happened, or why."

She walked the length of the trap. "Twelve men can die here at once? That's outrageous. The law. I guess I'll never understand the law."

"You don't have to understand it, just obey it and live a normal life, and the law won't hurt you. The best law is when you don't know it's there."

She touched his hand. "You haven't said a word about it these last three days. But I know you're still worried about the old woman. I could say I killed her in self defense. She came at me first with a knife. I had to defend myself." She stopped and watched him, then caught his hand and they walked back toward the hotel.

"Yes, I know I went a little crazy with the knife. She was dead and I knew she was dead and I went on stabbing her. Rage and fury were boiling out of me. They had kidnapped me, kept me. They had killed my parents. The old man had raped me and trained me to be a whore. The old woman had used me sexually when the old man was gone. They had robbed me of my youth. Suddenly a fourteen year old girl was a dance hall prostitute. I guess I'm not quite so angry at them any more."

Spur felt some of the tension draining from her. "Good, I'm glad you talked about it. Now it shouldn't bother you at all anymore."

They walked toward the hotel.

"You're not going to turn me in to Judge Parker?"

"What for?"

"The old woman who . . . died."

"What old woman?"

She smiled and they walked along in silence for a ways.

"Thank you. I'm not sure why you're being so nice to me. You'll probably attack me one of these times." She grinned. "Why don't you come up to my room and we can talk about books, and literature. You haven't told me yet when you're going to be heading out of Fort Smith."

"Tomorrow. After the hanging. The train will be through here at two in the afternoon. I telegraphed our office in St. Louis that I was testifying at the trial today."

"Oh."

"Nothing else to say?"

"I could plead with you to stay. I could ask you to marry me and take me with you. I could cry and plead and try to seduce you. But I'm not sure any of it would work."

"Tonight I'm going to start teaching you how to play bridge. A lot of the better people play the game. It's much more intellectual than whist or poker. I think you'll like it. Bridge is more socially accept-able than poker."

"Can we have some wine and cakes in my room while I learn?"

"Of course. Now, I better go see Judge Parker's clerk, and then send one more telegram. I'll be back to take you to supper, or dinner if you prefer, at

5:30. That will give you time to pick out a dress to wear tonight and then to lie down and have a short beauty nap."

"You think I need it?"

"No, but even perfection can be improved upon," Spur said. He kissed her forehead, then her cheek and slipped out the door. He tried not to notice if she locked it.

FIFTEEN

When Spur got up at dawn, he heard a bedlam outside his window. The street was filled with farm wagons, buggies, surries, cabriolets, and people on horseback. The flood moved slowly toward the courtyard . . . and the hanging.

He saw two three-seat full platform wagons that had more than a dozen people in them. There were road wagons, open buggies and rigs with tops and side curtains. He spotted one cut under extension top surrey with real leather seats and silver embossing on the sides of the seats that must have cost a small fortune. Two prancing blacks pulled it and a man and three women rode in it like they were royalty. For all he knew they might have been a prince or princesses from somewhere.

He washed, shaved and hurried downstairs. He found Irma standing on the hotel steps watching the show.

She grabbed his arm.

"All this for the hanging?"

"Right. It's been in the newspaper and word of mouth travels fast. Some of these people must have been driving for two days to get here. It will be a real celebration."

"To see five men die?"

"Not really. It's a celebration of law and order. They want to believe that this hanging will make them a little safer. That law and order and right will be more important and more possible now. It will pass, but for this time in this area, I think this kind of public hanging spectacle is a good thing."

They watched wagons filled with families drive by. There were blankets for sleeping, hampers and boxes full of food, and camping gear for outdoor cooking.

"Want breakfast first?" he asked.

Irma pretended to vomit, laughed and shook her head. "I couldn't eat a thing. I'm afraid I might throw it up when the trap drops."

They moved to the boardwalk, went down three blocks, then crossed the street with a dozen other people. They had to challenge the wagons and buggies to get across.

The courtyard was nearly packed already. No rigs had been allowed in to make more room for people. Some sat on blankets, but most stood waiting patiently. Spur and Irma squeezed into a free space.

"It's going to be over two hours yet before the hanging!" Irma said. "Look at all the people."

"There will be five thousand here before the trap springs," Spur said. They stood there watching the others. Talking from time to time. She caught his hand, then slipped her arm around his waist.

"This afternoon?" she asked looking up at him.

"Yes. I have to go. I have a job and duty calls."

"You could go deaf for a day or two."

"Could, but better not."

They watched young boys and a few girls climb

the walls around the old fort to get a better view.

In a roped off section right in front of the gallows stood fifty chairs. They were for the press. Reporters were there from St. Louis, Kansas City and Chicago.

The men on the fourth estate began drifting in, showing special papers to the deputy U.S. marshals at the gate and were escorted to the special chairs. The mayor of Fort Smith came with his entire family and sat just behind the reporters.

Soon the area inside the walls was filled and no more were let in. Wagons drove up along the walls and whole families stood on the wagon boxes to see.

By nine o'clock the sheriff and his deputies were on hand to control the crowd. It took some doing. The people were getting impatient. Babies began to cry. Mothers hurriedly nursed them to quiet the hunger pangs. Children became lost, screeching in fear and anger until a parent was found.

"Remember this," Spur told Irma. "You'll probably never see five men hanged at one time again."

"Lordy, I hope not!" Irma said and grinned at his expression of surprise.

At nine-twenty, Judge Parker's chief deputy and the U.S. marshal came out. They led a small line of men. Behind them came four ministers and a Catholic priest, then the five men who had been condemned. There were twenty rifle packing guards walking with the procession.

The U.S. marshal read the death sentences for each of the men. Then any of the five who wanted to was given a chance to speak.

All five were guilty of two or more killings, all unprovoked, and all done in the Territories for gain. One man who killed his friend for his purse and horse had nothing to say. The second man was being hanged for killing his wife and two children. He spoke for five minutes bewailing his mispent life and asking forgiveness. The marshal had to escort him back in line to stop him talking.

No one else spoke. The Jamisons snarled at everyone they saw, laughed at the ministers and priest and called them charlatans, hypocrites and worse than the devil himself.

The clergy offered prayers for the souls of the men, then led the throng in singing two religious hymns most of the crowd knew: *Rock of Ages* and *Nearer My God To Thee.*

When the last notes of the slightly off key hymn ended, a hush spread through the crowd. For a moment there was not a voice raised, not a baby's cry, not an animal whickering.

Two deputy U.S. marshals placed a black sack-like hood over each of the doomed men's heads and tied it around the chest. Then each man was led to his place on the trap.

George Maledon, the chief executioner, was a thin man with a full white beard and moustache, sad eyes and thinning black hair. He went to each man, placed a hand-woven, well-oiled Kentucky hemp rope around the man's neck and adjusted it exactly right so the heavy knot with thirteen loops around it would break the victim's neck the second he hit the bottom of the rope.

Maledon was a specialist, some said the best hangman in the country. The job had to be done right, otherwise the hanged man would twist and turn and die slowly of strangulation.

Maledon was often heard to say that he had never had to hang a man twice, and he never would have to.

When he had the fifth and last doomed man's noose properly placed he went back to the end of the gallows.

The hush that had affected the crowd intensified until the very silence could be felt.

Without any signal or announcement, Maledon sprang the trap.

The five killers dropped to quick broken neck deaths.

Spur let out his breath. He had no idea how long he had been holding it. He looked down and saw that Irma had dug her fingernails deep into the flesh of his arm. Three places showed traces of blood. She never knew she did it.

She gripped his arm tightly, staring at the swaying, black hooded figures on Judge Parker's famous oak gallows.

There were no cheers, no shouts. The crowd was stunned by the shock of the deaths. Families gathered and drifted away. The men of the press scribbled on pads of paper, looking around, then staring again at the slightly swinging figures before them. A few went to talk to the judge, others found Maledon the executioner and tried to get him to talk about his job. He turned them all away with a sad stare and a wave of his hand.

Spur guided Irma from the courtyard. She had not said a word since the hanging. Her hands both gribbed his arm. He felt her leg touching his as they walked. For a moment he sensed that she shuddered. Spur looked down at her. It had been a mistake to bring her here. She had seen her share of violence and death up close, ten times her share.

The crowd moved in near silence to the street and along it on various routes to get back to their rigs or homes. The bars and saloons were strangely quiet when Spur walked by them. No one was gambling.

From experience Spur knew that it would take two or three hours for things to get back to normal. By noon the gambling halls would be overflowing as everyone began to give his version of the hanging.

Spur found his way through the crowds to the boardwalk and then as quickly as he could to the hotel. He steered Irma straight to the second floor and into her room. Once inside she threw her arms around him holding him so tightly he thought she was going to crush him.

"Easy, easy, Irma. It's over now. It's all over. You never have to think about it again."

"No!" she screamed. "I want to remember it, always. It was the most thrilling, most exciting thing that has ever happened to me. I saw five men die at once!"

She reached up and pulled his face down and kissed him. Her mouth was open and she drove her tongue into his mouth. As she held him she stumbled backwards, then fell on the bed dragging him with her.

"Oh, yes! Yes! Right now while I still feel that jolting, that sound as the men all dropped at once!"

She tore at her dress, ripping buttons, pulling her bodice open, tearing the chemise off until her breasts were bared.

"Right now, Spur! Right now! I have to have somebody make love to me! Right now! Don't waste time!"

She pulled at his fly, ripping it open, digging inside for his genitals.

Spur lifted up, saw the wild, frantic look in her eyes, and knew that he had to humor her. He pulled his pants off and lay on top of her. Her hips beat a tune against his. She pulled his face down to her breasts and he ate his fill. Then she turned him over so she lay on top, pulled her tattered dress off over her head and quickly kicked out of the soft silk underwear she had bought only the day before. She lay on him, naked, her legs spread wide, her hand urging his turgid member toward her crotch.

Spur felt her need, sensed that this was somehow tied in with the rawhiding. She might never be rid of the violence, the death and how it was all tied up with the sexual act.

Then she had thrust him into her and she rocked and bounced on top of him. She climaxed almost at once, and he saw how it reduced her tension. She kept moving and two minutes later she shivered and the tremors rocked through her. This time she shrieked until Spur got his hand over her mouth. She writhed and jolted longer than Spur could remember her doing before, then she sagged on top of him. But when he tried to move her away, she shook her head.

She pumped him again and again, then slid down and took his penis in her mouth and played with his balls until he could not stop and jolted his load into her mouth.

She nodded, and then lay beside him, her arm around his shoulders as they rested.

A few minutes later she lifted up, pushed her breast into his mouth.

"Again, damnit, fuck me again! I need it again!" She turned over and held out her arms. Her knees came up and she screeched at him. "Spur McCoy you make love to me right now!"

He saw the frantic glint in her eyes. Why had he taken her to the damn hanging?

He soothed her, kissed her, moved over her slowly. He wasn't ready yet, but she solved that quickly with her hands. She pulled on him as he began entering her, then she sighed and relaxed and let him move at his own pace.

She climaxed again, and then again. Spur thought she would never stop, but at last she did and just as quickly she closed her eyes and her breathing became spaced, deep, even.

She was asleep!

Gently he came out of her and lay beside her. She slept on. Spur got up and dressed silently, then pulled a sheet over her and tucked it in around her shoulders.

Spur thought back to the rawhiding. Remembered how the women had argued over who "got this one first." So it had happened before. They captured a man, robbed him, the women fought over him, made love to him, and then what happened? Spur felt a shiver roll through him.

He remembered what the old man rawhider had said when Irma had been making love to him in the Territories. He asked Irma if she was ready yet. Ready for what? She had said no, she "wanted to keep this one for a while."

This one.

Keep this one for a while.

Then Spur remembered that the old man had held a six-gun in his hand. When Spur looked up the .44 muzzle had been pointing directly at his head.

Had they worked out a routine where the old man shot Irma's lover while he was still coupled with her?

Spur shivered. What had the old man done to this beautiful young girl? The hangings must have brought it all back. She had a strong tie between sex and death.

Would the compulsion fade, would a loving, strong man wean her away from any memories of those terrible two years in the Territories?

He stroked her golden hair and she reached out in her sleep and caught his hand. She brought it to her lips and kissed it, then put it over her breast. Spur left it there.

She woke up an hour later. Spur had not moved. She smiled.

"You've dressed already? Don't you have time for one more?"

"No. I have to get packed."

"That was wonderful, our making love. I don't care if anyone here knows. I just don't care!"

She sat up, careful to keep the sheet over her breasts. She looked down and laughed. "That is silly, being modest now." She deliberately lowered the sheets showing her breasts.

"Please stay longer."

"I can't. But I'll stop by to say good bye after I'm all packed and checked out. The train comes at two this afternoon and it won't wait. We have a couple of hours. Do you want to have lunch or dinner?"

"Yes," she said.

"I'll be back in half an hour."

He slipped out, sold his horse and saddle at the livery, paid his hotel bill and checked out with the judge's assistant. Then he took the most beautiful girl in the world to dinner at the hotel.

They talked of everything and nothing. He could see her becoming more and more tense.

Spur touched her arm.

"Irma, you're a lovely woman, a fine person. I know you're going to be very happy here. Go to church, join the choir and get to know the people. Men will be smashing into each other in three months to marry you. Wait and see. Forget all about me, about the Territories and everything that happened there. Start over, start fresh, and enjoy life."

He reached over and kissed her cheek.

"Now I have to hurry to the train."

He stood and watched her.

"Spur McCoy, I'll always remember you," she said. Then she smiled one of her perfect, beautiful smiles. "I hope you will remember me too. Somehow

I think you will."

He touched her hand, paid the bill and went to check out. His one small carpetbag was packed and ready.

Spur looked off the railroad coach at the small town of Fort Smith. Soon it would be only a memory, of a broken arm, a wild ride down a river filled with death and white water, and the capture of all that was left of the Jamison bank robbery gang.

And Irma Woodhouse.

He would never forget Irma. Such a beautiful girl. But such a tremendous problem. He wondered how she would do in Fort Smith. As the train lurched and pulled away from the station, he hoped that she would find a kind man, settle down and never be anywhere near to death or violence again. He had a feeling she would no longer want to go to the hangings in Fort Smith.

Spur settled down to the "jake" train ride that would eventually put him in St. Louis. It had been a year since he had been back there, since he had visited "his" office and talked to Fleurette Leon, the half French green-eyed blonde sweetheart who also was related to his boss in Washington D.C. He would worry about that when he got there.

Two days, the ticket man said. By the time they jigged and jagged across the state and then moved up toward St. Louis and the main line, they would have eaten up most of forty-eight hours.

Spur tried to relax. The cast was bothering him again. Yeah, it was itching under there! Why hadn't modern medicine developed some way to stop a cast from causing the skin to itch?

He went toward the dining car, found a "club car" where he could get a drink. It would help him stand the low grade but continual pain of the broken arm. He deserved it. Just one little drink.

He got a pair of beers and went to a seat next to a

202

window. The country slid by, and after a half hour it stopped being interesting, and picturesque, or even educational.

Face it, the country was dull.

He looked up from his beer and at a blue sheer silk skirt that must be on a woman who was standing next to his small table.

"Mind buying a girl a drink?" she said.

Spur looked up, then jumped to his feet.

"Irma! What are you doing on the . . . I thought you were going to stay back in . . ."

She sat down. "Sorry about surprising you, but even as a little girl, I always liked surprises, for me or on me." She looked at the two bottles of beer beside him.

"You drinking both of those, or could a lonely girl talk you out of one of them?"

He pushed the beer to her and set up his unused glass beside the bottle.

"Hi, Spur McCoy. How is the arm?"

"Fine, yeah, just fine."

They stared at each other. She took a drink of the beer from her glass. He tipped his bottle. They went through the ritual again.

"Sorry about the hanging. I shouldn't have taken you."

"No, no I wanted to go. I knew that something was rattling round in my skull. I wanted to see what would happen." She covered her face with both hands.

"Lordy, did I find out what happened!"

After a moment she looked up and smiled. "It's all right. I think I know what's going on. I have tied the two up for so long, and I was so young when it all . . ." She looked out the window. "I can handle it. I know what to stay away from. I can avoid those experiences, and then I won't . . . won't go all to pieces that way . . . I mean I can handle it now."

"We don't know that for sure, Irma, do we?"

"No, not for sure. I may never find out for sure, because I will avoid problems like that, situations, places where . . . like that. It won't be hard."

"You decided not to stay in Fort Smith?"

"Yes. It's too close to the . . . to the Territories." She looked up at him. "I thought St. Louis would be a good place to start over again, or just to start."

"Hope it works for you."

"Won't you be there?"

"This is the first time I've been back to St. Louis in almost a year."

"Oh." She finished the beer. "Well, would you walk me back to my seat?"

"Of course."

They went into the first car, then to the second. She stopped in the car that had been divided into compartments, small rooms, with the walk way at one side of the car instead of down the middle.

She used a key and opened the door. "This is my seat. Come on in."

Spur laughed. "Going in style, I see."

"For as long as the money holds out." She sat on the bed made up for two. "There is one bit of my education I am lacking. I hoped that you would help me one last time."

"Anything I can do."

"I have never really been seduced. I don't know what a man is going to do. I promise not to help, not to protest too strongly. I just want you to show me what happens, what a man does when he tries to get me to . . . you know, go to bed with him."

Spur chuckled and walked to the door.

"The first thing they do is lock the door, so no one will bother them. Probably the next thing would be a kiss." He sat beside her on the surprisingly soft bed and kissed her lips. She kissed him back.

"No, hold it, no helping. You would not kiss back

when you were not interested in the man. Let's try it again, and this time try to get it right.''

Spur kissed her and she sat without reacting.

"Yes, better, much better. He'd try to kiss you four or five times, then he would try to touch your breasts.''

Spur kissed her again. After all, he had said he would do anything to help her. It was tough duty, but he had to keep his word. Spur slid back on the soft bed a little farther, kissed her and against her gentle protests slowly leaned her back on the bed. Then he kissed her again.

It was forty-five hours to St. Louis. They would find some way to while away the time.